Steady Mobbin' 2

Marcellus Allen

Lock Down Publications and
Ca$h Presents
Steady Mobbin' 2
A Novel by Marcellus Allen

Marcellus Allen

Lock Down Publications
P.O. Box 870494
Mesquite, Tx 75187

Visit our website
www.lockdownpublications.com

First Edition December 2018
Printed in the United States of America

Lock Down Publications
Like our page on Facebook: Lock Down Publications @
www.facebook.com/lockdownpublications.ldp
Cover design and layout by: **Dynasty Cover Me**
Book interior design by: **Shawn Walker**
Editor: **Christina Blue**

Stay Connected with Us!

Text **LOCKDOWN** to 22828 to stay up-to-date with new releases, sneak peeks, contests and more...

Submission Guideline.

Submit the first three chapters of your completed manuscript to ldpsubmissions@gmail.com, subject line: Your book's title. The manuscript must be in a .doc file and sent as an attachment. The document should be in Times New Roman, double-spaced and in size 12 font. Also, provide your synopsis and full contact information. If sending multiple submissions, they must each be in a separate email.

Have a story but no way to send it electronically? You can still submit to LDP/Ca$h Presents. Send in the first three chapters, written or typed, of your completed manuscript to:

LDP: Submissions Dept
Po Box 870494
Mesquite, Tx 75187

DO NOT send original manuscript. Must be a duplicate.

Provide your synopsis and a cover letter containing your full contact information.

Thanks for considering LDP and Ca$h Presents.

Dedication

I would like to dedicate this book to my younger brother, Jacques Montgomery. Without you, none of this would be possible. It has been numerous times when I wanted to give up, but I thought about all of your sacrifices. You're truly my biggest support. I love you, brody!

I would also like to dedicate this to any fan who's ever had blood in their eyez! Family turning their back on you, friends leaving you when you need them… I share the struggle! This is for you.

I would also like to dedicate this to my CEO of LDP, Ca$h, for believing in me and being patient and real with me at all times, and my editor, Christina Blue, for making this series better than it would have been. I truly appreciate you.

Marcellus Allen

Chapter 1

"Turn it up some, baby," I told Tamia. The music got louder in my ear.

"You want me to start it over?" she asked.

"Naw," I said, then pressed the phone against my ear tighter.

Murder rap, we beat it, two a.m. in two-seaters
Yellow thing's bright embrace, I arch it back and lay
Face down, I'm a gangsta, my heart colder than Chicago
This black Impala just sent bullets through my car door
These niggaz I've been runnin' wit', pressure hit, they crumblin'

"You have one minute remaining," the hating-ass operator said, fuckin' up my flow.

I was getting my daily dose of music, usually Kevin Gates. That's how I stayed up on the music scene. Shit, that was my only method for the past three months, calling Tamia and having her play music over the phone for me. What a life!

Them crackaz came and threw me downtown as soon as the doctors said I was in the clear. They didn't even give me time to heal properly. They bitch-asses had me in booking with blood in my eyes, literally. I was arraigned on a murder charge, plus a felon in possession for the smack, and couldn't get bail until my hearing, which was next week.

"You about to call back?" Tamia asked.

"Naw, I'ma tap in later, baby. Love you!" I responded.

"Love you, too," she said right before the phone hung up.

I sat there by the phone for a minute, debating who I was going to call next. That's what my days revolved around, talkin' on the phone or playing chess with the ol' heads. I fucked with a few niggaz on the unit, but I kept to myself for the most part. The Multnomah County Detention Center was notorious for niggaz jumping on real niggaz's cases and for niggaz wearing wires.

Every time I turned around, somebody was complaining about how somebody else just jumped on their case. Them snitch-bitches be doing it real smooth, too, playing their cards right. They would post up all day with niggaz and talk about their cases, then next thing they got moved off the unit outta the blue. Days later, the nigga would be on the attorney phone getting served the news. What a dirty game.

"Hello?" Olay answered the phone sounding like she was busy.

"What's up, baby?" I asked her.

"Nothing." She was being short with me.

I inhaled real slow, then breathed out, trying to maintain my composure with the bipolar bitch. "Where's my son?" I asked.

"I'm not with him right now. He's with my sister."

"Then what are you doing?" I asked, feeling myself getting jealous.

"I'm going to practice, Marshawn! Damn!" she raised her voice with an attitude.

For some reason I didn't believe her ass. Ever since she moved to California she'd been acting real strange. I let her move my son down there while I fought the case since I couldn't physically protect them, but she knew whenever I touched down my li'l nigga was coming back. Me and her weren't on the best of terms, but she was still my bitch. Period.

"Yo, who the fuck is you raising yo' voice at, nigga?" I caught myself checking her.

"You, nigga! Calling my phone, asking all these questions and shit. Call ya other baby mama with that shit!"

she yelled, then disconnected on me.

Stupid bitch! I thought to myself. I hated when bitches played the phone game while niggaz were locked up, but I knew I was just one of thousands of real niggaz who felt this way. The only difference between me and most niggaz was I didn't need a bitch!

I'm self-made! I reminded myself as I walked into the TV room. I calmed myself down, then took a seat at the table with a few of the niggaz I fucked with.

"You done caking, nigga?" Tone asked as soon as I sat down, making us all laugh.

"I wasn't caking, nigga," I declared.

"Stop lying, nigga. I seen you with the phone hella pressed to yo' ear, and you was hunched over," he shot back, thinking he had me.

"Blood, I was listening to my Kevin Gates, like I do every day," I responded.

"You sweat that, nigga. He ain't even hot like that," Tut jumped in the conversation.

"Nigga, you sound drunk, and yo' favorite rapper is Joe Blow. He don't compare!" I shot at his ass.

"What?" they both yelled at the same time, then Tut said, "Blow will rap circles around that nigga."

"Mozzy would, too!" Tone threw out there.

"Both those niggaz rap about the same shit every single song. My nigga Gates does it all. He touches every topic and kills it!" I had to inform those haters.

"All that nigga does is sing and cry about the bitch!" Tone falsely accused.

I screwed my face up, looking at both those niggaz like they were retarded. "That's how I know you just talk to hear yourself talk. He definitely doesn't."

The Unit Deputy called my name, saying I had a legal

visit and cutting our conversation short.

"We gon' finish this when I get back!"

My mind was runnin' wild while I waited for my lawyer to come inside the visiting room. He had called the day before saying he had some really good news and some bad news. I stayed up all night tossing and turning, tryna figure out what it was. That shit drove me crazy, especially with the way my mind worked. I always analyzed everything, always tried to plot and plan everything, but now that I was in a jail cell, didn't none of that shit matter. I was on state time.

"Hey, Marshawn! How are you holding up?" my lawyer, Ryan O'Donald, greeted me as he came in and sat down.

The first thing I noticed was the stack of papers he sat down next to his laptop. *Aw shit,* I thought to myself. "I'm good. Just ready to get up outta here and hear about this news you have," I said while watching him power up the computer.

"Okay, let's start with the bad news first. There's actually two parts to it."

My heart dropped as soon as the words left his mouth. *Two parts?* I wondered to myself. My mind instantly went to me doing life in a fuckin' cell.

I started hearing my song *War Pain* playing from his computer and was confused on why the hell that was relevant to my case. I made sure my facial expression matched my thoughts as I scrunched my shoulders in a 'so what?' manner. Then he switched to my song *100 Shots* before he answered my unspoken question.

"So, the State is alleging that in your songs you're rapping about how you're going to kill certain people, and then you rap about it after you or your friends did it. They sent me over five songs and a few videos of you and your friend to back their accusations," he told me while I was watching the music video.

I knew exactly where he was going with this shit, so my mind instantly started looking for ways around it. I started analyzing every bar and their exact meanings. It was bad, but I damn sho wasn't about to fold.

"What does my music or any of this shit have to do with my case? I'm only charged for this murder and nothing else. You've already told me we're going the self-defense route so everything else is irrelevant. They're just reaching," I defended my cause.

He took the computer and started pulling something else up. "Which leads me to the other bad news they just threw at us." He stopped talking while he dug through all the paperwork he brought in. "Alright, they have a confidential informant, and he states y'all have had multiple shootings between each other. He claims he's a member of your rival gang, and you've personally killed some of his friends. He gives times, dates, and dozens of shooting for both sides. He claims the beef is over drug territory and you had a hit out on Tyrone Johnson."

I interrupted him right there. "That's a lie!" I raised my voice.

"Which part?" he asked, then studied my face to get a read on me.

I thought about lying and denying everything like I was trained to do, but decided to keep it real with the man I needed to save my life. *Shit, I'm paying him over a hundred bands,* I reasoned with myself.

"I ain't never put no hit out on that dude. That's a lie. We were beefin' and all that, but it was more over personal shit than drugs, at least on my end. But like I said, self-defense. He came to my home to kill me, period."

"What about the songs?" he asked.

"I never said I was going to kill him specifically, and I'm

not charged with nothing else," I clarified again.

The more I made my case, the more I convinced myself of my so-called innocence. A nigga couldn't tell me nothing. I was gon' beat my shit.

"Alright, time for some good news, which I believe is the key to the case," he said, turning the computer around.

I watched the video and felt the evils runnin' through my veins as I watched Gucci Ty make his entrance through my gates. *Bitch-nigga,* ran through my mind as I mugged the screen. I saw him drive through with no problem at all. *I'ma kill that gatekeeper,* I promised myself. The next shot showed him driving in the parking lot, then he disappeared.

The screen went black for a few seconds, then showed me walking down the hallway in a rush. It showed me get on and off the elevator, and then it went blank again. I didn't understand the good news part at all. We already knew I lived there and the nigga didn't, so what? Then he made me understand.

"Go look at the time stamps. You see how he got inside an hour before you even walked into the hallway?"

My heart started beating faster as I found the time stamp he was talking about. I looked at it, then compared it to the one with me in the hallway. "Yeah, I see it now!" I said, starting to understand what he was getting at.

"Now, here's the even better news. For the whole hour window, he never leaves the parking lot."

"Because he was waiting on me," I finished his sentence, finally getting it.

"Exactly my point. Now, I got something for you to really think about, and this is important." He closed the laptop and leaned in closer to me. "How bad do you wanna get bail, and how bad do you wanna beat this case?" he asked.

14

I initially felt like that was a dumbass question until I leaned back and thought. I knew what he was really asking me. "Not enough to start snitchin'. I already told you that. We agreed not to even have this conversation," I checked him, feeling my temper rise.

"We're not having it. I'm talking about something different."

"A'ight then! Then I'll do anything to get outta here," I gave in.

"I want you to testify on your own behalf. Not just at your trial, if it makes it that far. I'm talking about at our bail hearing next week. Trust me, they won't see it coming, especially at the hearing," he broke it down to me.

My mind started racing as I processed what he wanted me to do. I weighed the pros and cons. "What would I have to say?" I asked.

"It's simple. Just that you guys had some type of music beef and it was never real to you. On that fatal morning, he must've took it personal and came to kill you. He shot first, and you defended yourself," he told me.

I pictured how it would play out in my mind over and over. *This shit could work*, I told myself. The only thing I was worried about was the D.A. questioning me about other shit outside of the case.

"The D.A. can only question about this case, right? No other shootings or murders?" I needed clarification.

"With bail hearings, the state gets more leeway than at trial. For instance, hearsay is admissible at the hearings, but don't worry about that because I'll object to whatever is not related to this case. This is your life here, Marshawn. If we lose trial, you get life," he reminded me.

I wanted to go home like a muthafucka, but I damn sho wasn't about to be doing no dry snitchin' or none of that shit.

My reputation meant the world to me. I knew about a whole lot of shit the State would love to know. Plus, I didn't know if tellin' on a dead man was snitchin' or not.

"Let me think about it overnight," I said, then started going through the papers he brought in.

"What's up with all this shit? Anything important?" I asked.

"Just a bunch of gang crap that won't matter in trial: ballistic reports and stuff. It is some interesting stuff in there, though, far as ballistics go. The State wants to connect you to a string of gang shootings, and they plan on doing it with their informant and ballistics reports," he broke down to me.

"How the hell can they do that?" I asked, confused as hell.

"Motive and opportunity. They'll claim you killed him because of y'all's ongoing gang war."

"This some bullshit! He came to kill me, so where they getting this dumb shit from?" I was mad as fuck hearing how the pigs was tryna get at me. I really wanted to find out who the fuck was their C.I. That nigga had to die.

"Last thing. Two detectives, Rogers and Freeman, claim you came to the homicide scene of your friend Boobie and made threats. The next day Mr. Johnson is killed, and ballistics match the casings from Boobie's death to two other ones they claim you're involved in," he informed me.

That made absolutely no sense, but my heart was pounding out of my chest just hearing that shit. *Ballistics?* I wondered. "What other shootings?" I asked while tryna dig it out of the paperwork.

"One from the night your friend died, and the other was outside some house. Go through it all and fill in the dots for me next time. Think about what I said about our defense, too," he said, then stood up, hitting the call switch.

My mind was still on that ballistic shit and what that meant for Boobie's situation. Then something popped into my head right before he left. "I thought the police had to actually have the gun in order for them to match the casings?" I asked.

"To be 100% sure, they do. You'll see in there that they have quite a few of them. Call me when you're ready," he said right before the guard escorted him out.

Hours later, I was sitting on my bunk with a heavy heart and a headache outta this world. I had to wipe away a few tears that were threatening to fall down my face. I checked the report for the fifth time praying it would change. It didn't. The same 9mm that killed Boobie was not only used twice that night, but on another night I remembered vividly.

According to the ballistics report, fifteen 9mm shell casings were recovered from a homicide scene on 82nd Flavel Street on June 30th. This same gun killed Boobie, simple as that.

One of my own niggaz killed Boobie.

"Fuck!" I screamed out, then jumped up, throwing the papers everywhere. I paced for hours trying to remember who had the 9mm that night. Burnside or Joe? I even tried to think of any alternative theory. I came up blank. There was no denying the logic, no getting around the science.

Every memory started flooding my brain at one time that had something to do with Joe and Boobie beefing. All the hate. All the arguments, the fight. I played the scene over and over again in my head and couldn't believe how bad I fucked up. The first words out of Joe's mouth was, '*I'ma kill you for that.*' The look on his face was dead-ass serious.

It was blood in my eyez and evil in my heart as I thought of multiple ways to kill that man. I couldn't believe the heart of that nigga. It made me wonder. *Was Burnside in on this shit?* I asked myself. My head was all fucked up. I didn't know what to think. I knew nothing was going to be the same. Lines had been crossed.

As I lay in my bunk later on that night, I finally let the tears come outta my eyes. I was fucked up beyond anything I'd ever felt in my life.

I woke up in the middle of the night sick to my stomach. I had been wrong. Burnside had the 9mm that night. I remembered it clear as day.

I didn't sleep the rest of that night. It was blood in my eyez.

Chapter 2

I had been listening to the bitch-ass D.A. lie to the judge and crowd for over an hour. Not only was he lying, but he had ho-ass gangstas on the stand doing the same thing. They were putting on a real monkey show, and the shit was irritating the hell outta me.

"I know it's hard. Trial is even worse," my lawyer whispered in my ear and rubbed my shoulder.

I knew what he was getting at, but it was pointless 'cause my mind was already made up. I was getting on the stand and playin' that role, period. One thing I learned in jail was everybody in there was losing. I don't care how much money a nigga's worth, if he can't spend it freely, then he's losing. Plus, I couldn't wait to revenge Boobie.

Fuckin' traitor, I thought to myself.

I ended up blocking everything out until my lawyer told me to get ready. The first thing I heard was the D.A. finishing his speech about how their informant was so reliable. *I'ma kill his rat ass when I figure it out*, I promised myself.

My lawyer talked a li'l bit, then told the judge I'd be testifying. Everybody started talking loud, making the judge bang his gavel to get it back quiet. Nobody was expecting to hear from me, especially the D.A. It was written all over his face. Surprise.

After I got swore in and went through a couple bullshit questions, my lawyer got to the real reason we were there.

"Mr. Anderson, did you know Tyrone Johnson?" he asked me.

"Yeah, I knew him growing up," I answered, then looked at his homies in the crowd. Them bitch-ass niggaz were tryna mug me and look hard.

"Were you guys friends?" he asked.

"No," I said a li'l too fast.

"What would be the proper title then?"

"I would say enemies," I replied while staring Pressha right in the eyez.

He made a gun with his fingers, then shot me. It always amazed me how niggaz claimed to be hard, then showed up for court dry, snitchin' and shit. Wearing the niggaz' face on the shirt for the judge and the jury. *Niggaz be killin' me.*

"Why were you guys enemies?"

"We grew up on opposite sides of the city. But I never took our personal beef serious, outside of music," I replied.

My lawyer paced back and forth like he was deep in thought, then turned back to me. "If it was never serious, then why was Mr. Johnson killed outside your residence?" he asked the million-dollar question.

It was all eyes on me at that very moment. I usually love the spotlight, but this was a whole 'nother monster. I locked eyes with Burnside for a long moment. *Traitor*, I told myself.

"He came there to kill me for whatever reason he had. He said 'it's time to die,' then started shooting at me," I said, only telling half the truth.

The crowd got loud for a minute, then died back down. Those Gutta Squad niggaz were shaking their heads at me, and Pull-Out mouthed '*snitch*.' I couldn't wait to get out and torch those niggaz.

"After he started shooting first, what did you do next?" he asked, leading me on.

"I started shooting back and running away from him. Eventually I fell and blacked out. I didn't know what happened until I woke up in the hospital."

"Did you want to kill him?"

"No, I was just tryna defend myself. I was on my way to meet a friend, not get shot at." I laid it on thick.

"So, you weren't meeting Mr. Johnson?"

"No," I answered.

"Had he ever been to your home?"

"No, sir."

"How did he know where you lived?"

"I don't know," I said. I felt my blood starting to boil at that question. I stayed up many nights asking myself that shit. I had a pretty good idea, though. *Your own kind wants you dead*, was Gucci Ty's last words. That shit never left my mind since that morning.

"Okay, let me show you this video and see if you can identify some things for me," my lawyer said, then started playing the surveillance tape.

Everybody's eyes were glued to the TV, anxious to see what trick my lawyer had up his sleeve. We watched Gucci Ty pull up to the gate and talk to the nigga in the booth for a second, then slide him some money before being let in. I reminded myself to kill his ass in the worst way.

"You recognize him?" my lawyer asked.

"Yeah, that was Mr. Johnson paying to get inside of my condo."

"Objection! Hear-say and speculation," the D.A. jumped up.

"Overruled. Save it for the trial," the judge replied, looking irritated he had to speak.

"Can you read the time, for the record? The time at the bottom."

"It says 9:01, sir," I answered.

Then he played the video of me walking down the hall, headed to the garage. I smiled inside, knowing where he was going.

"Is that you?" he asked.

"Yes, sir," I replied.

"Can you read the time, for the record?"

"It says 10:09, sir."

"Do you usually keep your friends waiting for over an hour that's coming to pick you up?"

"No, I don't, and he's not my friend," I said just how we practiced it.

"But he was waiting in your parking garage for an hour?" he said.

"Because he was waiting to kill me, like I already said," I played victim.

"No further questions," my lawyer said, then sat back down.

I looked around while the bitch-ass D.A. gathered his notes. I could tell he was surprised and hella frustrated. *Oh well, fuck his bitch-ass*, I thought as I made eye contact with Tamia. I couldn't wait to take those county blues off and fuck my bitch.

"Mr. Anderson, are you a Blood?" the D.A. asked.

He caught me off guard a li'l, but I was well prepared.

"Yes, sir," I answered, looking him dead in his bitch eyes.

"Was Mr. Johnson a Crip?"

"I believe so," I answered.

"Have you ever been shot or shot at by the Crips?" he called himself baiting me.

"I've been shot and shot at, but I don't know by who," I replied.

"You and Mr. Johnson been in any other shootings with each other?"

"This was my first time shooting at anybody, sir," I tried to hold in my smile as I lied.

For the next ten minutes he kept asking the same shit over and over again just in different ways. All he proved was I was a gang member and made some hard-ass songs. Our surprise attack worked like a muthafucka. I knew I was getting bail, and so did everybody else. I could feel it in the air.

After he was done proving nothing, him and my lawyer gave the judge their closing arguments, and we were dismissed for afternoon break. I nodded at my niggaz as the punk-ass guards escorted me outta the courtroom.

One hour and a nasty-ass lunch later, they had me back in the court to hear what the judge had to say. A few bitch-ass niggaz mugged me and mumbled some slick shit. Whatever!

"You think we got action?" I asked my lawyer soon as I sat down.

"I think we're good, but you never know with this judge," he whispered back to me.

The bailiff told everybody to rise for the cracker judge, then we sat back down and awaited the decision.

"I usually like to take a few weeks to decide a murder case, but in this situation, I'll be making a ruling today. I've paid close attention to both sides, and I'm more than convinced the evidence thus far backs Mr. Anderson's claim of self-defense."

The crowd got loud the second he spoke those words. Most people were cheering for me, but I heard a few groans, too. I instantly turned around, smiling at my mother and Tamia.

"However, I am concerned about some sort of retaliation in the gang community, as the Gang Task pointed out. So, I'm setting bail at $500,000. My ruling is final," he said, then stood up to leave as the crowd got loud again.

My heartbeat sped up at the thought of my return to the streets. It was time to raise the murder rate dramatically, starting with my own niggaz. I locked eyes with Burnside as

I walked out. He nodded at me like he was a real nigga. I smirked at 'im. *That's yo' ass, boy*, I promised myself, then made my exit. Fuck-niggaz! I felt nothing but betrayal and murder in my heart. I couldn't believe it, out of all niggaz.

***

I stepped outta that dirty-ass jail the next day feeling untouchable. I inhaled the fresh morning air and stood still for a minute. I saw Gotti's white Benz parked across the street, but I wasn't in a rush at that moment. I knew once I hopped in the car, my life as I once knew it was gon' be over. It was like walking into the Matrix. There was no going back.

I exhaled real deep, then walked across the street, ready for the world, ready for the war. The crisp October air smacked me in the face as I made my way to the car. I welcomed the cold air. It matched how I felt inside: cold, sharp, and unforgiving. It felt abnormal walking around outside without my vest on. I felt helpless and vulnerable. That muthafucka saved my life multiple times, and I needed it. Especially since I wasn't fully healed from the last gun battle.

"What's mobbin', nigga?" Gotti greeted me, sounding all happy and shit.

"Ready to get some pussy and then go purge. Take me to Boobie grave sight first," I replied, then grabbed the bag off the backseat. I pulled out the clothes he'd brought me and changed right there in the front seat. Black sweats, black hoodie, black gloves, and I was coo'.

"Glove box, Blood," he told me after I put the gloves on and started looking around.

I pulled the .45 out, cocked it back, then leaned the seat back. "A'ight, let's hear it. All of it," I said after preparing myself mentally for the bullshit.

"What you wanna hear first? It's a lot to tell," he asked sounding like life was really beating him down. Either that or he had some shit to tell me that he really didn't want to.

"Let's start with my money. How the fuck I get hit for a hundred rackz?" I growled, feeling my temperature rise.

My mind went back to the day Tamia visited me and told me the short message from Gotti: I lost a hundred thou. I was so hot it messed the rest of my visit up. All I could think about was my money. I'd lost a li'l over $300,000 since I caught the case, including lawyer fees. I had to get back on my grind.

He shook his head. "Niggaz hit yo' spot in the Piedmonts and got lucky. They probably figured since nobody be in there that it was a stash spot or sumthin'. They just got lucky, Blood," he told me his theory.

Or it was a inside job, I thought to myself, but decided to keep it to myself for the time being.

"That nigga, Twin," was all he could say, then started shaking his head slowly.

Damn, it's like that? I wondered. I knew the li'l nigga had been trippin' hard, but I didn't think it was that bad! Twin was Boobie's younger brother who grew up in Atlanta, but had moved back to the town to wreak havoc behind his brother's death.

"You sound like you can't control the li'l nigga or somethin'. He only 23," I teased.

"Man, that li'l nigga is a fuckin' headache and an urban terrorist! He don't care about shit except for killin' behind his brother. He on some broad daylight or in the mall type of shit. He don't give a fuck!"

I laughed at my nigga, then put back on my murder face. That was my first time cracking a smile since I read the ballistics report. *Just the type of nigga I need around me,* I thought as I got back in beast mode. For the shit I had planned, we was gon' need all the shooters we could get.

I felt a wave of anger mixed with sadness wash over me as we pulled into the cemetery on 60th and Freemont. I rubbed my eyes behind my glasses to try to prevent the tears from spilling out. *I can't believe this nigga gone,* was the thought running through my mind. I couldn't understand how my main nigga was with me one day and I was visiting his gravesite the next. It's a dirty game.

"What's poppin' with those Murda Squad niggaz? They on their trip?" I asked, then opened the door. The wind hit me hard, reminding me to stay cold inside.

"They been trippin' a li'l bit, but not as much as everybody expected," he replied, further proving the theory I had in my head. Fuckin' snakes.

I nodded my head slowly. "Figures," I commented, leaving no doubt I felt some kind of way.

"You sound like you know somethin' I don't know," he caught on.

"I do," I admitted, then dug in my pockets, pulling out the ballistics report. I handed it over. "Read this while I visit with my nigga. I need some one-on-one time, anyways. That shit gon' blow yo' mind, Blood," I told him, then jumped out, closing the door behind me.

I stuffed my hands inside the hoodie, grippin' the pistol with both hands while I walked to the last place on earth I wanted to be. I always knew this game was built on death, but for some idiotic reason I never imagined Boobie getting killed. He was too gangsta, too hard. But I was wrong.

It felt like the longest walk of my life, but when I finally made it to the tombstone, I broke down. I couldn't stop the tears from pouring out of my eyes even if I wanted to, so I just let 'em fall. Seeing the pictures of my bro as a li'l nigga on the headstone brought a pained smile to my face. "My nigga was loved," I mumbled.

It started drizzling rain like even God had to shed a few tears for the realest nigga who was now lying in a box. *Is this some type of omen?* I wondered. I chalked it up to typical Portland weather and wiped my eyes with the back of my hand. *No more tears,* I promised.

"What's mobbin', nigga? I just came here to let you know in person I know who killed you. I still don't really understand why, but that question ain't never mattered, anyways. Man, Blood, I can't believe that nigga Burnside would violate like that. Yo, I'm not coming back until I revenge you, and that's on you. It's blood in my eyez," I said, then stood there staring for a while.

I pulled my phone out and logged on to my Snapchat. "The king is back, so you bitch-niggaz already know what time it is. Y'all might wanna start buying y'all Christmas presents early, 'cause I doubt you pussies are gonna make it. I'm back." I mugged the camera, then aimed it at the tombstone for a few seconds before I posted it and headed back to the car.

The walk back was ten times faster than the walk to the grave, probably because I was on a mission. I had a purpose. I was gon' kill some niggaz.

Marcellus Allen

Chapter 3

"Now it's all startin' to make sense! Fuckin' snakes!" Gotti yelled out, pacing back and forth like an angry lion stalking its prey.

It was usually me and Burnside who was losing our cool and Gotti tryna calm us down. I looked over at Twin. He was staring at the ballistics report like it had poison on it. Originally I was going to keep all the information to myself until I knew how I wanted to play it. I don't like to rush into nothing without thinking everything through first, but I felt like I woulda been wrong for holding back something that deep. So I went against my better judgment and called a li'l meeting at the Mob Quarters to confess what I knew.

"What's startin' to make sense?" Bleed asked, sounding uninterested. He was never the one for too much talking, just straight action. He was sitting on the couch rolling a blunt, real calm. Too calm.

"Nigga! How Joe and Falon been on some Jay-Z and Beyoncé type of shit, thinkin' they the new king and queen of the city. How Burnside and Joe been acting like they in charge of the family now, and why they flew their cousins down from Jersey to run shit for them. They on some hostile takeover type of shit!" Gotti broke it all down.

I sat back, listening, taking it all in and weighing his words with caution, looking for any flaw in his reasoning. I saw none. *Damn, Burnside, say it ain't so,* I prayed for him.

"Fuck you mean they been having their family run shit?" I asked after I got done analyzing every word he said.

I remembered Gotti coming to visit me and telling me Burnside wanted to send for his two relatives. Something about they were too hot in Jersey and could come down here and help us out.

"They've been having their cousins, Beast and Premo, overseeing all the trap spots and collecting all the money. Then, when it's time, they turn it over to Burnside or Joe, then one of them brings it to me," Gotti relayed to me.

The more he spoke, the angrier I became. It was all starting to make sense now. Just like Gotti said. *I've been played,* were the words running through my mind. I instantly got a headache thinking about all the money that had probably been stolen from me.

"Blood, you know how much money could have been stolen from me?" I spat, feeling my blood start to boil.

"Yo' money?" Twin screamed while jumping off the couch with his pistol dangling at his side. "Yo, dawg! My muthafuckin' brotha lyin' in the ground, and you worried about yo' money? Nigga, fuck yo' money!" He looked me dead in my eyes as he said it, too.

Take a deep breath. I know what I'm doing. I had to calm myself down. I bit my lip while I forced my anger to settle down. I looked him up and down, taking him all in. Dark-skinned, about 5'9", li'l dreads on his head and ready to die. He looked and acted like Boobie so much it was crazy. He was hurting and had been in Atlanta for too long to fully understand the danger he was in.

"Listen, Blood, lower yo' muthafuckin' voice," I said in a deadly tone while standing up. I got right up in his face so he could read my eyes and get a glimpse of the evil that was lurking in my soul. *Dis ain't what you want,* I thought to myself.

"Ain't nobody in this room love your brother more than me, and that's on Bloodz. I love you like a li'l brother, but the next time you disrespect me like that with a gun in yo' hand, you better kill me. Understand?" I checked his li'l ass.

He didn't respond with words, but when he stuck his gun

back on his waist, that was enough for me. A tear slid down his face while he tried his hardest to maintain eye contact with me. I pulled him in and held his face into my chest as he silently cried.

I stared at Bleed for a few seconds. He just shook his head. I looked over at Gotti. *I know how to tame the wolves,* my eyes told him.

"On Shady Park, we gotta kill those niggaz. All those bitch-niggaz!" Twin yelled, then stepped back, looking me in the eyes for confirmation. I nodded my head. "Even Burnside, right? That nigga ain't innocent in this shit, dawg. He gotta get it!"

Hearing those words caused mixed emotions to run throughout my body. Part of me wanted to defend my nigga, part of me wanted to kill him. I was hoping he had some reasonable excuse that would allow me to spare his life.

I looked at Bleed and Gotti. They were staring back at me, no doubt waiting to hear what I would say.

"I know it was Burnside's gun that killed yo' brother. That means he did it. I don't fully understand why, but we gon' get to the bottom of it. That's my word, li'l bro," I gave my oath.

"Fuck gettin' to the bottom of it. Let's go kill dem fuck-niggaz tonight!"

"Naw, we gotta wait to see how deep this shit goes or else it's gon' happen again. We gotta rock these niggaz to sleep. That means playin' coo' like we don't know what's up."

The look that appeared across his face let me know exactly how he felt. He wanted to kill immediately. He was ready to purge.

"C'mon dawg–"

I cut him off. "Look, Blood, I understand how you feelin' right now. I need you to understand this shit is deeper than our emotions. I'm responsible for people's lives and their families' lives. We gotta move right," I broke down to him. *I'ma have to keep this li'l nigga close to me,* I decided right then.

"Here they come right now," Gotti said, standing by the surveillance monitors.

I looked at Twin, giving him the look to stay calm. He sat down on the couch and pulled his phone out, texting. *Good,* I thought. I felt my heart tryna pound out of my chest. *Take a deep breath. I know what I'm doing,* I had to calm my inner beast.

"What's mobbin' with my nigga?" Burnside yelled, then came over to give me a G-hug. I hugged him back, and that's when I sized up the two niggaz standing behind him who I'd never met before. They were both tall and skinny with matching bald heads and beards. Their whole demeanor screamed East Coast. I could just tell. I didn't know why those niggaz were in the building, but I damn sho got to it.

"Shit, you know, steady mobbin'! What's up with these niggaz, though?" I nodded in their direction.

"Oh, these my relatives," he ushered both of them over. "This is Beast and his younger brother, Premo. We flew 'em in from Jersey."

I shook 'em both up outta respect, but I wasn't feeling their thrill. Far as I knew, they were a part of some type of infiltration conspiracy.

"What's poppin', son?" they both said.

Great, two more Jersey Joes. "What's mobbin' wit' it?" I returned the greeting, then turned to Joe. "What's good?"

"Shit, son, you know. Getting' money and reppin' that five. I'm glad you out, though, son." He made his way over to give me a G-hug.

I couldn't put my finger on it, but somethin' was off with

the niggaz' energy. I was gettin' bad vibes. Call it a gut feeling.

After everybody shook each other up, it was time for us to have a meeting. That meant it was time for niggaz to leave. "Yo, Beast and Premo, no disrespect, but I'ma have to ask y'all to leave so we can have a li'l meeting," I said.

They both had stupid-ass looks on their faces like they were genuinely confused or somethin'. I don't know what the fuck they thought, but they damn sho wasn't staying for that. I didn't know those niggaz. They looked at Burnside.

"Yo, O, these niggaz is family right here. Let 'em stay so they can be filled in on everything," Burnside spoke up.

What the fuck? Is this nigga crazy? I had to ask myself. That nigga must've really thought he was in charge or somethin', but I was gon' cool his ass down.

"They might be family, but you know how this shit goes. I only hold meetings with the top four niggaz, that's it. It's been niggaz in our family for years that ain't never been to a meeting, and you know that. No disrespect to yo' family right here, but I'm not about to discuss certain shit in front of them. I just met 'em," I laid down the law.

I didn't give a fuck how they felt. It wasn't no way I was discussing murders with them niggaz. Plus, I needed to establish who was in charge and break up their li'l circle of power. I was onto their li'l game.

"Yo, son, what's the difference between them and this li'l nigga right here? Since he's Boobie's brother, that makes him special?" Joe jumped in.

Twin had been doing his best to stay calm like I asked, but that comment put him over the edge. "Yeah, that makes me special. You got a problem?" Twin jumped in his face.

"Li'l nigga, you must don't know how the fuck I get down," Joe shot back, never the one to back down.

I saw everybody slightly reaching for their guns. The line was being drawn in the sand.

"Y'all fall back off that dumb shit. We all on the same team in here," I demanded.

"You sure? 'Cause it don't seem like it," Burnside replied. He was looking from Bleed to Gotti to Twin, then back to me. He could feel it in the air, or was it his guilty conscience?

"You testing me, Blood?" I asked, then got right in his face. Now I was mad. He knew better than to question my authority like that.

"Naw, you got that," he backed down, knowing he was wrong.

"I love you, my nigga, but there can only be one head. I made the decision to replace Boobie with his li'l brother. We good on that?" *He wants to be the head,* I thought as I stared into his pitch-black eyes.

"Yeah, we good, nigga," he responded a li'l too aggressive for me.

I'ma have to kill this nigga sooner than I wanted to, I told myself. I couldn't believe the predicament I was in, all of my niggaz plotting on each other.

"Why don't we just cancel the meeting until tomorrow so we can let temperatures cool down," Gotti suggested.

"Yeah, let's do that," I agreed, then walked off to my back office. I had to get away before I killed all those niggaz. My anger was rising to its max level, and I didn't know how much more I could take.

After my frenemies left, I ended up going back out to the front so I could see how my real niggaz felt and let 'em know what my plan was. If I wasn't convinced 100 percent before, I was by that point. Them niggaz were plotting on me. All of them! It was coo', though, 'cause I had somethin' real special planned for those pussies.

I dapped everybody up after letting them know we needed to link back up the next day. Tamia was blowing me up, and I hadn't had no pussy in three months.

It took us 45 minutes to get to the new house I had gotten for Tamia while I was locked up. She kept on complaining how she felt scared to even walk through the parking garage at night. I couldn't have that shit, so I gave her the down payment for a new house and she chose one in Vancouver, Washington. We pulled up to the two-story home on Fourth Plane Avenue and killed the engine.

"I can't believe it done came to this," Gotti said, shaking his head. We had both been dead quiet the whole ride, deep in our own thoughts. We knew the road that lay ahead was a long and treacherous one.

"I did too much thinkin' in that cell. We didn't cause this shit. They did. I'm 'bout to go get some pussy tonight, and we kill tomorrow. Somebody's gotta die. That's just how it gotta be," I declared, sounding more cold than I actually felt.

"Say that, then," he said, dapping me up.

"I just did," I replied, then hopped out and headed up the stairs.

As soon as I walked into the front room, my dick instantly got hard. Tamia was waiting for me on the couch, butt-naked with her legs spread apart, playing with her pussy. She took her fingers out, then stuck them in her mouth, sucking them real slow. She never broke eye contact.

"Come taste your pussy, daddy," she purred while opening her legs wider.

I took my clothes off, then dove right between her thighs. She was already so wet it made no sense. Her stomach was showing now at four months pregnant, and I assumed that's where the extra wetness had come from. I went to work on her clit first, sucking it, then blowing on it.

"Oh! Daddy!" she moaned while gripping the side of my head.

I kept on attacking her clit for a few minutes, then got to sucking on her pussy like it was the sweetest thing I'd ever tasted. When I stuck my tongue in her pussy, she got real animated.

"I'm about to cum! Oh, it feels so good!" she screamed.

I stuck my middle finger in her ass and started lapping her insides with my tongue until she nutted all over my face. She wrapped her legs around my neck and arched her back while I finished eating up all the juices spilling out of her.

"Okay, I'm done!" she yelled and tried to push me off of her.

I locked onto that pussy and went even harder. She was screaming and moaning out a whole bunch of shit I couldn't understand. I just kept on licking and slurping her until she started shaking and cumming in my mouth for the second time.

"Ah! Oh! I'm done, daddy!" she yelled and panted.

"You done now?" I came up from the pussy with her juices dripping off my face.

"Yeah, let me suck yo' dick," she pleaded.

"Hold up!" I said, then started eating her ass out.

"Oh! Ooh!" she moaned.

I was going all out for her that night. I wanted her to know I appreciated her holding me down like a real bitch. She was going to get the best of me. I continued to eat her ass until I was tired of her begging me to stop.

"You ready for this dick?" I stood up with my dick pointed straight at her.

She leaned forward, grabbing my meat and smiling like she was the happiest woman on earth. "I've missed you," she spoke to my dick, then started kissing it real slow everywhere. The she licked the whole length while keeping eye contact with me.

"Stop playin' with me, Tamia," I told her, gripping the back of her head.

She opened wide, stuck her tongue out real dramatically, then put the whole dick in her mouth inch-by-inch. I think I started seeing stars. It had been months since I had some head, and I was definitely on cloud nine.

"Ah, shit!" I moaned out, standing on my tippy-toes.

Slurp! Slurp! She sped the pace up, really going to work.

"Argh, fuck!" I gripped her hair and started controlling the rhythm. The more I felt my dick touching the back of her throat, the badder I wanted to bust in her mouth. By the way she was sucking and slurping, I could tell she wanted the same thing, but I wasn't ready to nut yet. I wanted to cum inside that pregnant pussy, so I slowly pulled out, causing a popping sound.

"Why you do that?" she whined.

"Turn around so I can hit that pregnant pussy. You know what's up!" I demanded.

She smiled, then stood up, turning around real slow, teasing me. She bent over, grabbing the edge of the couch. "Like this? Or like this?" she said, then put her knees on the couch, arching her back and giving me the money shot.

I slapped her on the ass. "Like that." Then I entered her from behind. It was so wet and warm I had to stop on the third stroke. I was afraid if I stroked one more time, I was gon' blast off already. I needed to catch my composure, but Tamia wasn't going for it. She started throwing her huge ass into me, doing the work herself. I gave in and went back to work.

"Daddy! Daddy! Oh, I missed this dick so much," she

moaned.

I slapped both cheeks at the same time, then watched them jiggle back into place. I gripped each cheek, then started digging in. "Argh, fuck!" I growled out involuntarily. The pregnant pussy was on a whole 'nother level. I promised myself I'd keep her ass as pregnant as possible while I was shooting off in her.

"Ah, shit!"

Chapter 4

Halloween

I was fresh outta some good pregnant pussy when I got a call from Twin telling me to check my Facebook and Snapchat. I had almost hung up on the nigga for calling me that late about some social media shit. I was ready to start round three with Tamia. What the fuck? Then he told me hella niggaz were calling me all types of snitches on there.

My blood started boiling while I was scrolling through all of the posts and comments about me. Somebody had even managed to sneak a picture of me while I was on the stand. They were pushin' a hard line on me. *I'ma kill these niggaz,* I declared while gripping the phone harder.

I couldn't believe muthafuckaz were putting a jacket on me. *All the shit I done did? A real nigga ain't never walked these North-East Streets!* But then again, this was Portland we were talkin' about. Muthafuckaz put jackets on real niggaz eight out of ten times. If you beat a case, you're a rat. Make bail, you're a rat. But if you're really a rat, these same muthafuckaz will make excuses for you or claim they "ain't seen the paperwork." That's their favorite one. If there is real paperwork, all a nigga gotta do is push a hard line on the enemy and his homies would forgive him. Just don't tell on the homies!

"How you wanna do this, dawg?" Twin asked from the driver's seat.

After I started seeing red from all those disrespectful posts, I jumped outta the bed and told Twin to suit up. Thirty minutes later we were sitting in his black Impala, parked around the corner from Sam's Bar off 162nd and Stark.

"She said those niggaz in there deep, right?" I asked. I

was tryna come up with a good strategy on the fly.

"Yeah, it's about ten of those fuck-niggaz in there. They getting ready to hit the after-hours in a minute, though," he replied.

"Fuck it then, Blood. It's Halloween, so let's give those pussies somethin' to be scared about. Pull into the lot, then we gon' sit on 'em 'til it's time to purge."

"Say less," he said, then pulled into the semi-packed parking lot.

I got to looking around immediately for any enemies I could find. I wanted to find one of those Gutta Squad niggaz, but we didn't have the line on them yet. But that was coo', 'cause the Piru niggaz were just as guilty in my eyes. *Your own kind wants you dead,* Gucci Ty's last words echoed in my head. I stayed up many nights tryna crack that riddle. *How the fuck a Piru nigga find out where I lived? I should go dig Gucci Ty bitch-ass up and ask 'im,* I thought to myself. Ever since then I'd been feeling like the world was against me.

"That's the nigga Danger car, right there," I pointed and whispered like somebody might hear me. I knew that red Monte Carlo from anywhere. Plus, it stuck out like a muthafucka wherever it was. Danger had it sittin' on 26" rims, TVs all through the car, and the insides were cocaine white. He like to show off, and now it was gon' cost him.

"Yeah, it's an open spot right across from his ho-ass. It must be what God wanted," Twin said while parking directly across from the car. We were facing his front, just waiting for his ass.

"Naw, this is the devil's plan, right here. God ain't got nothin' to do with this," I corrected him. I always tried to keep God out of my evil deeds for some reason. Even though I knew I was a killer and was going to hell fo' sho, I could never commit blasphemy. Never! I don't know, maybe deep down in my heart I felt like God would have some mercy on my soul.

"Yeah, dawg, they say Halloween is the devil's night. I don't give a fuck whose plan it is, somebody dyin' tonight. And that's on Zone 3," he declared.

I just nodded my head at the truth. Somebody was gonna die.

"I'm not about all these niggaz throwin' dirt on my name," I broke the silence after five minutes. I also wanted to hear his opinion on it, too.

"Real niggaz ain't going for that, shawty, real shit. Fuck these fuck-niggaz. Plus, half they homeboyz be certified rats, anyway. You made a power play that any smart nigga would make," he lectured me.

It felt weird listening to a li'l nigga give it to me raw like that, but that's exactly what I needed. I got pumped up with each word. I couldn't wait to purge. I looked over at my best friend's li'l brother and I swear it felt like Boobie was sitting next to me for a second. I just hoped his gun game was like his brother.

Thirty minutes later those suckaz finally decided to show their faces. They came out being extra loud and stumbling while they walked. It was about seven or eight niggaz plus a few bitches walking with them. I recognized all of them niggaz. I used to consider them my homies. My heartbeat sped up with each step they took. I knew what time it was. The nigga Danger wasn't the one speaking on me on the net, but some of his li'l homies was. He was gon' pay the price, though.

"You ready, nigga?" I asked, then slid on my Freddy Krueger mask.

He grabbed the AK off the backseat, cocking it back

before answering. "This what I do, dawg."

I smiled behind the mask. *Just like his brother*, I thought. "You gon' put yo' mask on?"

"Naw, I'm bare-face on this one, shawty. I'm 'bout to torch these fuck-niggaz," he replied.

We watched their group start to break up, headed to their own cars. I was gon' let everybody else get away, then changed my mind. I gripped the Mac 11 with anger from just seeing them pussies.

"Soon as him and the bitch get in the car, it's go-time. You chop him down and I'ma torch the rest."

"Say less," he responded.

I watched Danger yell out to his homie DJ, then hop in his whip with some light-skinned bitch. I kept my eyes locked on DJ and the li'l nigga he was standing with. *Take a deep breath. I know what I'm doing.*

"The Mob back, nigga!" I screamed out as soon as I jumped out, waving that Mac.

Boom! Boom! Boom! Boom! Boom!

The li'l nigga grabbed his chest and folded up instantly. DJ took off like the bitch he is, but I was on 'im.

Boom! Boom! Boom! Boom!

I shattered a car window tryna take his head off. "Naw, nigga, don't run now!" I yelled, taunting him.

Yoppa! Yoppa! Yoppa! Yoppa! Yoppa!

That 'K started going off, and I already knew what that was about. I was looking for the scary nigga when glass shattered from the car next to me.

Boc! Boc! Boc!

"What's brackin', nigga!" some nigga from their hood yelled out after dumping on me.

I turned around, facing him and letting my gun talk for me.

Boom! Boom! Boom! Boom!
Boc! Boc! Boc!

We were both shootin' and runnin' in between parked cars. I didn't recognize the young nigga, but I could respect his gangsta. He was going toe-to-toe with the best to ever do it. *Where is DJ?* I wondered while still shootin' it out. I had too much experience to fall for the old distraction trick.

Seconds went by before I watched a car pull out of its parking spot. I thought it was some innocent people tryna get away until the passenger window rolled down and DJ stuck a gun out, aiming right at me. It all happened in slow motion. For some reason, probably fear mixed with surprise, I froze up for a split second. That second could've cost me my life. Once I saw the flash of the muzzle, that snapped me out of it. I ran sideways, returning fire.

Boc! Boc! Boc! Boc!
Boom! Boom! Boom!
Boc! Boc!
Boom! Boom!

They drove off slow with DJ hanging out of the window. I got to bustin' back from behind a parked car.

Boom! Boom! Boom!
Boc! Boc!

We exchanged shots until we both felt like the other was outta range. "Bitch-ass niggaz," I mumbled to myself.

Yoppa! Yoppa! Yoppa! Yoppa! Yoppa!

I heard that instrument of death again and took off toward the sound. What I saw was some shit straight outta one of those hood books or a mob movie. The nigga Twin was standing on the hood of Danger's car, shooting at DJ and his homie as they drove by. All I saw was fire jumping outta that barrel. *This li'l nigga crazy,* I thought, then started shooting, too. I didn't wanna feel left out.

Boom! Boom! Boom! Boom!

Twin hopped down after those bitch-ass niggaz darted outta the lot. He was mad they got away. It was written all over his face. Shit, I almost didn't recognize his face. He'd changed. He didn't need to wear no scary mask, his face was a mask. All I saw was determination, murder, and the devil. He had devils in him. *Just like me and his brother.*

We locked eyes, one killer to the next killer. I looked around him to the car and saw Danger and the bitch slumped over. The windshield was shot out. He had jumped on the hood and crushed them. *Cold.* I don't think me or Boobie would've thought of that move. I nodded my approval of his gangsta to 'im. He nodded back. No words necessary.

Our moment was broken up by the sound of sirens and the moaning of the nigga on the ground tryna crawl away. *I thought I killed him?* We looked at each other, then ran over to his bitch-ass.

"I should let you bleed out to death, pussy!" I yelled, standing over him after I kicked him in the ass.

"Awe, c'mon, don't do me like this. I don't wanna die," he whined like the bitch he was.

I hated when grown men cried like hos. We all knew what we signed up for when we joined this shit. It was all fun and games until it was time to get off Snapchat and really pick those guns up.

"That's the only guarantee in life. Yours came sooner than expected," I gave it to him raw.

Boom! Boom! Boom!

The Mac opened his chest up to help free his soul. He was no longer with us.

"Fuck-nigga!" Twin said, then kicked the shit out of him.

Somethin' wrong with this nigga, I thought while shaking my head at him. We broke back to the car and got the fuck up outta there. When we were in the clear, I couldn't hold it in any longer. "You need counseling, brody," I said.

"I need my brother, shawdy," she shot back.

I didn't know how to respond to that one.

***

After we handled that li'l trip, I went straight back to Tamia's spot and slept like I didn't have a care in the world. Fuck those niggaz. I woke up to my dick in Tamia's mouth, blew her back out, then hit up the studio. I wrote so many songs while I was in County I could've dropped a whole new mix-tape that day, but none of them felt right for the beat Ruger had playing for me. Most of the songs I wrote were on some deep, depressive type of shit. This beat was calling for me to talk shit on it. That's what I planned to do.

"I'm almost done, Blood," I told Ruger.

"Take yo' time, my nigga. We can't rush this shit," he said, then hit the blunt a few more times before passing it to me. "We gotta capitalize off your buzz as much as possible. We gotta strike hard these first couple songs."

I hit the purp a few times while I thought about what he was saying. I could drop the real songs later on, but for the time being I needed to dig in those pussies' chests. I needed to drop that real street shit. Let 'em know it was war. I was gon' take the same route Mozzy did: destroy my enemies on wax every chance I got. That was gon' keep me relevant and gaining new fans. Then I was gon' drop some real shit for my core fans.

"Yo, I'm 'bout to scratch the hook and change some shit up," I told Ruger.

"Oh yeah? What you thinkin' 'bout doing? You look like you up to somethin'," he asked.

"I was just thinkin' about what you were just saying." I hit the blunt one more time, then passed it back to him. "I need to capitalize off my buzz right now, off the situation, off my name. I need to stay standin' on niggaz' chests while I drop a new mix-tape. I'm 'bout to change the name of the song, too," I told him.

"Change it to what?" he asked.

I thought real hard, then came up with, "*Winter Time War*. Yeah, I like that shit. I'ma heat the winter up," I answered, real cocky like.

He nodded his head real slow. "What about *War for the Winter*? That sound more direct, more deadly and personal."

"Yeah, I can fuck with that. That do sound better. That's gon' be the first track on the mix-tape, right there. That's gon' set the tone," I agreed.

"What we callin' the mix-tape?"

"Blood in My Eyez," I answered without even having to think about it. My mind had been made up for months on that title. I read a book by George Jackson with that same title and had been stuck ever since. The whole book was about war, and that's exactly what was on my mind. The only difference was I wasn't planning no racial revolution. I was huntin' niggaz!

Thirty minutes and another blunt later, I was standing in the booth ready to deliver. It felt good being back behind the microphone. I was charged up! I promised myself if I made it outta the war alive, I was gon' start taking it more serious. It's amazing what sittin' in a cell can do to your mind. The beat dropped, and I was ready for it. Back like I never left.

"Yeah, I'm back, nigga! Out on bail on a body, fuck that dead nigga! Huh! Fuck all the local Portland Crip sets, too. Ain't no more, I ain't on it. Fuck all that! Fuck you fake-ass Blood niggaz, too, clickin' up with Cross Towns. Where they do that at? Fuck Gutta Squad. Fuck Rollin' 60's Crip. Fuck Murda Squad Piru. Fuck all those other mobs and squads that ain't with us! It's Mob up or get shot down, period. War for the winter, nigga. Lock your doors or get ya funeral money ready. The king back!" I spoke, real turnt up.

I was dead serious, and it could be heard in my voice. I looked at Ruger while I waited for the beat to drop again. We locked eyes. He nodded at me with a smirk on his face. He knew I was in my zone and shit was about to get epic.

Early confession, it's 30 shots in this chrome weapon.
Kill my enemies, stop baby mama from stressin'.
Ain't no feelin' like the first day outta County,
But on my head it's still 20 thou for the bounty.
Probably not, shoulda seen Gucci Ty dead in the parking lot.
His whole body spun three times before he finally dropped.
Heart big as a lion, shoulda known not to try 'im.
And that car Ron died in? That's a collector's item.
Yeah, my Mob nigga had to fold 'im up.
Pull-Out started cryin' when the coroner rolled 'im up.
That was for Trell, nigga. He gon' catch you in hell, nigga.
And Butta, I ain't stoppin' 'til ya head is on my shelf, nigga.
Half Dead, still a bitch, and Pressha, the boss of the click,
If you ain't have that li'l money, you'd be saucing his dick.
We going body-for-body 'til the weight get too heavy.
Boobie dead, we gonna war all winter. Hope you niggaz are ready.

I finished the verse and looked up to get a read on Ruger,

and that's when I noticed Burnside standing there. *When the fuck he get here? I gotta watch this sneaky nigga,* I wondered. He had a smile on his face and was nodding his head like he was really feelin' my shit. He raised both arms in the air to greet me. With one hand, he threw up the Mob, and the other was holding a cup of lean. I threw it back up, then jumped into the hook.

When it's war time in the winter,
Niggaz won't make it through the winter.
They say life's a bitch, well I'ma kill her.
I told my mama 'don't pray for a sinner
'Cause I'm catchin' bodies all winter.'

I did the hook a few times until we felt I had the timing down right, then I started diggin' back into those suckaz' chests.

They on Facebook throwin' dirt on a real nigga name.
I find it funny they still ain't get back Dirty Dan's chain.
Fuck Mike, fuck Floyd and fuck Smoke.
If them Bompton niggaz mad, I can make a call out to Figuero.
Fear no nigga, just kill mo' niggaz.
Halloween massacre, almost killed fo' niggaz.
We can't have no meets, we ain't squashin' no beefs.
Baby mamas ain't safe, li'l kids get the heat.
I ain't hard to find. I be on Haight Street
In a bulletproof Maserati, so these bitch niggaz hate me.
Mad that they ain't G, mad that they ain't me,
Mad I made bail, mad I remain free.
Half dead, a straight bitch, we ain't gon' respect yo' crippin'.
They shot up the barber shop, ain't hit shit but a few clippers
And it's body-for-body, nigga. It's gon' get heavy.

For Boobie, it's war all winter. Hope you niggaz is ready.
After I added a few ad-libs and did the hook again, I
stepped out to a smiling Burnside. He seemed genuinely
happy I was back recording and pullin' those niggaz' cards.
Snake muthafucka! I knew the worst type of enemy was the
one smiling at you. I couldn't understand how I had missed
all the signs.

"Yeah, Blood, you killed that shit! Them cowards gon' be
sick when you drop that shit. We gotta shoot a video for this
one," he said, all turnt-up while shakin' me up.

I felt like a sucka for shakin' him up, but I quickly
disregarded that thought and tried to hide my emotions. I
wanted to kill that nigga so bad.

"I'm about to torch them niggaz all winter, on the Mob.
In the booth and with the banger, I'm done playin', Blood.
Everybody gotta die about Boobie." I spat the last line with
more venom than I intended, but since I did, I watched his
eyes for any sign of deceit.

I saw none, only genuine hurt and anger. *What the fuck?
This nigga is good,* I started to question myself. Was I wrong
about him? *Naw, he had the gun. It was his.* I knew I was just
tryna find an excuse to spare his life.

"You already know what time it is, Blood. Yo' I heard
last night was our work?" he replied.

"Just a quick heart-check. I was mad about that hot shit
they were tryna say about me," I answered.

I felt myself getting mad from even talking about it. That
shit had me hot! I took my Gucci shirt off and tossed it on the
couch. Now I was shirtless with my .40 cal showing on my
hip. I started pacing the room, walking in circles like I was
still in that cell.

"Fuck what those bitch-ass niggaz are sayin'. Real niggaz
know what's up with you, and so do they. They just talkin' to

hear themselves talk," he said, coming to my defense. He sat on the couch and started sippin' his lean. He kept his eyes on me, tryna get a read on me for whatever reason.

"Yeah, you right, Blood," I said, then took his cup and got my sip on. It had been a while since I'd sipped the lean, plus being in County had my body back on it's natural course, so I started feelin' the effects within minutes.

It was dead quiet in the room. Ruger had his headphones on and was busy putting the finishing touches on the track. Burnside was sitting on the couch, watching me pace and sip outta his cup.

My phone went off, shattering the silence. I had to take a deep breath after I saw it was Olay. "Where the fuck is you and my son at?" I raised my voice, losing my cool. Her dumbass had been playing phone tag with me the day before, and the shit had gotten under my skin. Every time I called, she didn't answer, then she called back later when I was busy. I'd text her, then she'd take an hour to respond.

"We'll be there tomorrow. I couldn't make the flight for today," she answered.

"Ok, coo'. Mar-Mar don't know I'm out, right?" I asked.

"Naw, I ain't said nothing to him," she replied.

"A'ight, coo'. So, is you about to let me eat that pussy tomorrow, or what? I've been craving it for months," I said, then sat down with a smile on my face. I started sippin' while she went off.

"Nigga, please! You ain't never tasting me again, foul-ass nigga. You better call that dark-skinned, fake Spanish-talkin' bitch! You were probably fuckin' her all day yesterday, anyways. And don't think I'm stayin' at that house, either! I'm dropping your son off and leaving," she spazzed on me.

I was smiling the whole time. As long as I could keep her in her feelings, then I knew I still had her. I wasn't worried about those frivolous threats. "I wasn't fuckin' nobody yesterday, Olay. I've been waiting on you," I lied.

"Whatever, nigga. Fuck you and that pregnant bitch!" she yelled, then hung up on me.

I looked at the screen, shrugged, then tapped the syrup one more time.

"Aye, Blood, pass my shit." Burnside got up and snatched his cup back.

I wasn't trippin'. I was already on one by then, anyway. I looked at the nigga who was supposed to be one of my best friends and shook my head. After all the shit we had all been through, and he wanted to play it foul? I just couldn't understand why, but one of the main lessons Jaxx taught me came to mind: *Money and power will make any nigga turn on you.*

"I came over here to holla at you on some one-on-one shit, though," he said.

"What's mobbin'?" I asked.

"Shit, you tell me, brody. I don't know how to explain it, but yesterday yo' whole vibe was off. We just felt like you wasn't fuckin' with us for some reason," he had the audacity to say.

For some reason? This nigga was playing a dangerous game, and he was bold, but that was Burnside all the way and then some. If he wasn't nothing, he was dangerous.

"I'm not feelin' how you brought some new niggaz to our meeting. I don't know them niggaz, Blood, and to be real, I don't think I wanna know them. That shit rubbed me the wrong way 'cause it's protocol to this shit," I spat at him.

"You right, Blood. I shouldn't've brought them like that. It's just that they've been the main one's holding it down with us, and they wanted to meet you," he explained.

I bet! "I'll meet 'em when the time is right. Right now,

I'm just focused on killin' them suckaz and getting my money back up. We took too many financial loses," I said making sure he could feel my distaste. "I don't understand how niggaz can just walk in our spots and clean us out. No suspects or nothin', and it's coo' with y'all niggaz?" I felt myself getting hot.

"Hell naw, it ain't coo', nigga! I lost some money with that shit, too. Niggaz just got lucky and hit a good lick, Blood."

"I'd call stealing over a hundred bands a great lick, but fuck all that, my nigga. That spot was under your family's control. It's their problem. So, until further notice, they're out. I don't want them nowhere near my money. You better front them some work or somethin'," I spat, full of animosity.

He didn't like what I had to say, and he made it known with his body language. Like I gave a fuck. He screwed his face up while staring me down. The way his eyes got low and the quick flash of anger that rippled through them let me know he'd taken offense. He scooted up to the edge of the couch.

"Blood, you taking shit too far. I understand you don't trust niggaz, but this my family you talkin' about right now. I guarantee they had nothin' to do with that," he declared, sounding extra passionate.

"You willing to put yo' life on that?" I asked with more seriousness than he could know.

"Absolutely!" he stated.

"Good. Either way, they're still out when it comes to watching over my money. That's the way I want it." I wasn't budging on that.

"A'ight, my nigga. I'm gone," he said, then got up, giving me a weak-ass dap, then walked out.

I lay out on the couch, not giving a damn about his

feelings. *Fuckin' snake!* They thought they were doing somethin' while I was rotting in that cell, but them traitors were so busy playing offense that they forgot defense wins championships.

While I lay there staring at the ceiling, plotting my next move, one of my brother's constant war tactics came to mind. *The worst type of enemy is the one you don't know is your enemy.*

Marcellus Allen

Chapter 5

I had been standing by the window for close to twenty minutes watching everybody arrive when Gotti finally came to get me. We were at the house we referred to as the Mob Spot, or the warehouse on 8th and Bryant Street. I called an emergency meeting, which I never did, so I could get a feel for things. There's nothing like body language. Nothing. People could front all day with their words, but it was a whole other thing to lie with your eyes and energy.

I also wanted to show my authority and flex my muscles a li'l bit. I knew it was important to show my face every now and then to the bottom niggaz. The foot soldiers. Let them see I didn't think I was too good to be around them. Plus I knew it was gon' come a time where sides were going to be chosen. A line in the sand that could never be washed away.

"Why you just been standing there staring out the window like that?" Gotti spoke to me from the doorway.

I turned around and stared at him for a few seconds. He was the only nigga I knew who would come to a war meeting, one in the morning, dipped in designer from head to toe. I looked him up and down, then smirked. "You going to a photo shoot or a music video?" I asked, then smiled at the only nigga I trusted 100%.

He looked down at his red-bottom shoes, then his fitted jeans, and brushed off his tight-fitted designer shirt. "This ain't nothin' but my play clothes," he said real arrogantly while shrugging his shoulders. "But you in here on some straight bullshit. You look like Malcolm X with a bunch of jewelry on. Lookin' out the window all paranoid and shit," he said, then laughed at me.

I smirked for a second 'cause he did have a li'l point. I had on some black Tom Ford jeans with a bulletproof vest, no shirt. My pistol was in its hip holster, and I was heavy on the jewels. My platinum Presidential Rolex was shining bright, and so was the bracelet. I had my Jesus pieces on, plus my signature 'M' medallion hanging down to my stomach. I was on my bullshit. *Like Che Guevarra wit' bling on, I'm complex,* Jay-Z lyrics popped into my head.

I turned and looked out the window one last time. It was gloomy outside with the clouds getting darker by the hour, just waitin' to rain down on the city. I inhaled real deep, then exhaled. I knew exactly how those clouds felt. I was dyin' to make it rain in the town. I was gon' make it rain bullets, though. I couldn't wait to get rid of the dark clouds that were lurkin' inside me.

"Everybody ready?" I asked, changing the conversation.

"Yeah. It's that time," he answered.

"I'm on the way," I said, still staring out the window. My mind was still tryna solve the problem that was rackin' my brain. I knew I was only gon' get one chance to get this right. When I struck, I had to make it count, and that's exactly what I intended to do. *I can't believe I'm going through this shit!*

I made my way down to the basement five minutes later knowing exactly what I needed to do. When I stepped into the basement, all the small talk immediately stopped. It was all eyez on me. *This is power,* I thought as I made my way to the front of the room. It was a li'l over thirty niggaz in the room. Most of them I had only met a few times, but they all repped the Mob, and that alone meant the world to me. That was supposed to mean the world to them, also, but obviously loyalty was at an all-time low.

"I'm back. They tried to kill me, and that didn't work. They tryna give me a life sentence, and that damn sho ain't gon' work!" I yelled, then paused to let the words sink in. I looked every nigga in the room in their eyez. I needed to read them. "So yeah, I'm startin' to feel real untouchable around this bitch. The only problem is, shit that's around me has been getting touched. Trell got touched, then Boobie get touched, and we still ain't got no answers to that shit!"

I looked Burnside dead in his eyez to see if he would tell on himself. He didn't. I only saw pain and anger. *He's good.*

I looked at everybody else, then continued. "Then I go to jail and my money came up missing. Over a hundred thou. I guess some niggaz got lucky on a good lick, but I still ain't got no answers on that, either. So, now I'm startin' to get real suspicious. For now on I'm changing up the trap houses and the money collecting. Shit about to get real tight around here. But on another note, it's time to turn up. Since we don't know who exactly killed Boobie, everybody gon' get it! Gutta Squad, Murda Squad, Piru niggaz, Sixties, and whatever crabs and fake Bloodz is ridin' with 'em. We gon' celebrate my freedom on Saturday night. Wake up the Lord's day, go to church, spend time with ya family or what not. Once Monday hit, I want everybody in this room ridin' for a week straight. Shoot to kill, and I don't care who y'all purge on. Mob up or get shot down!" I yelled out.

I let the silence rule the air for a few seconds, then I walked out. Wasn't nothin' else to say at that point. It was time to eat. The whole town was food!

It took thirty minutes to drive to the airport to pick up Olay and my son. I was puttin' in work in my Maserati so I could hurry up and get there. I didn't feel like hearing Olay bitch about me being late, but the main reason was I couldn't wait to see my bitch and my son. Those two meant the world to me.

I ended up getting there a li'l early, so I put the new Kevin Gates mix-tape 'By Any Means II' in and listened to my nigga spit the ghetto gospel.

When I saw them coming out of the door, I hopped out with a smile on my face and open arms. My son dropped the li'l bag he was holding and sprinted over to me yelling, "Daddy, Daddy," the whole time. I scooped him up, kissing 'im all on the forehead, then pulled his mama in for a group hug. This was my family. I could feel Olay wanting to break away, so I gripped her ass tighter. She wasn't going nowhere if I could help it.

Once we got in the 'Rati, she started to put back up her walls, but I wasn't trippin' off that shit. I'd been dealing with her since she was a kid. I knew how to tear those muthafuckaz down! She had another thing coming if she thought I was just about to accept losing my bitch. Fuck that! We were gon' talk about this shit. A nigga had too many years invested in the shit to just walk away. Hell naw! Plus, she had my heart. Tamia was a good bitch and I loved her, but Olay had my heart. Period!

We got to my mother's house a li'l later, and she was happy as hell to see a nigga. She put me in a bear hug for, like, five minutes, then started complaining about me being in the streetz too much. Blah! Blah! Blah! I lied to her about getting out soon and shook to the background where my brother Jaxx was at, leaving the women to the cooking and shit.

Jaxx even had the audacity to tell me I should lay low for a while and stack my money up. I don't know what the fuck he had been smoking, but it must have been some rare shit, 'cause it had him trippin'. I told that nigga I hadn't even began to turn it up. By the time I was done, the punk-ass mayor was gon' have to call in the Feds and the National Guard! I was hurtin' inside, and I was gon' make sure everybody else in Portland felt the same. I told that nigga to just keep droppin' the work off like clockwork and fall back. Long as he gets his money on time, he good. Let me handle this street shit!

We all ate dinner like a happy family to please my mother, then got the fuck up outta there. I tried extra hard to get Olay to come up off the pussy that night, but she wasn't going for it! She even slept in the guest room to stay away from me. It was triv! I was mad about that li'l stunt, but had to remind myself I was the one who had fucked up. I chalked it up as her way of making me work for it. Whatever!

The next day I met up with Twin and Bleed after I dumped off three bricks to my Oakland nigga. Twin wanted to post up at the store his brother was killed at on 15th and Prescott Street, so that's what we did. We posted up in the lot on the side of the store right off Prescott so everybody could see us.

It was pretty cloudy outside, but not yet raining. The town was on fire, though, from over a dozen shootings since I pressed the button at the meeting. They claimed they was searchin' for me, so I decided to make their jobs that much easier. Fuck them niggaz!

"What's Mobbin' wit' it? Y'all already know who this is, and y'all already know what time it is. We out here on Fifteenth and Prescott not giving a fuck how y'all feel about it! It's supposed to be a war going on, but we outside sittin' on Maseratis and shit. I hope you bitch-ass niggaz come through," I talked my shit for the camera.

Bleed had pulled his I-phone out and started flexin' for Snapchat, so shit, I did the same thing!

"Oh, bitch-ass niggaz hiding in the house and shit. Fuck crabs, and if you a Blood and you fuckin' with the crabs, then you a slob, and I hate slobs! Mob life, nigga," Bleed jumped back in.

I looked at him like he was crazy for saying that 'slob' word, but that was the new thing nowadays. Bloods calling other Bloods slobs! I wasn't with that, though. Fuck that!

"Aye, shawdy, I'ma kill all you fuck-niggaz about my big bruh," Twin threatened in his southern drawl.

We put the video on Snapchat, then got back to kickin' it like we ain't have a care in the world. I was sittin' on the hood of my Maserati, hittin' the blunt, watching my surroundings. Smokin' weed in Oregon was legal now, so niggaz be getting high in broad daylight like 'fuck the po-po!' What was they gon' do?

We spotted a group of bad bitches walking into the store, and we planned on mackin' on as soon as they came out. It was Friday, so they were probably headed to get some swishers to get high before they hit the club up later on.

"Excuse me! You in the pink! Can I talk to you, beautiful?" I threw my arms in the air while I yelled over.

The group of women studied us for a second, then walked over to us looking badder than a muthafucka. It was five of them in total, and I wanted to taste them all. I hopped off the 'Rati real slow and swagged out, feelin' myself like a muthafucka. All of them were eye-fuckin' me, but I had my sights on the thick redbone in the pink. I could tell they'd never seen a street nigga pushin' a 'Rati, but there's a first time for everything.

"My name is O-Dawg. Can you tell me yours?" I spit at her while shaking her pedicured hands.

"Hi, my name is Crystal," she responded, showing me all her perfect, white teeth.

"You're beautiful, Crystal." I gave her my pearly whites now.

"Thank you. Um, is O-Dawg the name your mother gave

you?"

Jokes. "Naw, that's the name the streetz gave me, and it's my rap name." I gave it to her raw, then waited for the recognition to kick in. She looked over at her two friends who didn't get chose by my homies. The other two were busy getting macked on by my niggaz.

They gave each other a knowing look before focusing back on me. *It never fails,* I thought as I hit her with my signature smirk. "Oh, I know who you are. I love your music." She was all on my dick now.

"Especially the new one you just dropped dissin' everybody," her dark-skinned friend jumped in. By the way she was eyeing me and the 'Rati, I just knew she was down for the threesome.

We chopped it up with the bitches for another five minutes, got the numbers, and invited them to my party before watching them walk away.

"I'ma fuck that bitch after the function on the 'B' watch," Bleed boasted.

"Yeah, 'cause you gon' pay for it," I jabbed at 'im.

"You must got me confused with this trickin'-ass nigga from the south right here," he shot back, pointing at Twin.

While Twin was shootin' back at 'im, my eyez were focused on a black Escalade that had pulled up across the street. I didn't know what it was, but I just felt the evil vibes coming from the truck.

My cell phone ringing in my pocket made me break my concentration for a second. The name that came across the screen made my heart rate speed up. Bitch Butta.

When I looked back up, four niggaz had hopped outta the truck and were crossing the street. I instantly recognized my arch enemies: Butta, Pressha, Pull Out, and Half Dead. *Just the niggaz I wanted to see.*

I pushed Bleed out of the way with my left hand and started bustin' that .45 with my other.

Boom! Boom! Boom! Boom! Boom!

They weren't expecting me to start gettin' off the way I did. They thought I was lackin'. Never that! They spread out in the middle of the street, tryna avoid the hot slugs I was sending their way.

"This ain't what y'all want!" I screamed while runnin' sideways, tryna get behind a car.

Boc! Boc! Boc!

Boom! Boom!

Boc! Boc! Boc!

They started returning fire, tryna take a niggaz' head off. By that time Bleed and Twin had joined the party and it was a shootout.

We were clappin' at them and they were bustin' back! We were shootin' from behind cars, and so were they. It was so many bullets flying that neither side wanted to cross the street.

"Fuck slob life!" Butta yelled out while ducking behind a car.

"Fuck yo' dead homies!" I yelled back.

"Fuck Boobie!" one of them screamed back.

Boom! Boom! Boom! Boom!

Boc! Boc! Boc! Boc! Boc! Boc!

That shit sent Twin into a rampage like he was possessed by a demon or somethin'. He hopped up, clappin' his toolie while walking toward them.

What the fuck wrong with this nigga?

I figured he was ready to die about it, but I wasn't ready to see him go, so I jumped up, firing like my life depended on it. At least I had on my vest under my red Champion hoodie to back up my braveness. Bleed couldn't stomach being left out, so he popped up right behind me, bustin' his thang.

Boom! Boom! Boom!

My adrenaline was pumping so hard I could hear my heart pounding like it was right in my ear. We kept advancing and shootin' while they stayed ducked off behind cars like the bitches they were. It was bullets flying everywhere. I swear I heard a few zip by my ear.

All of a sudden Twin fell flat on his ass in the middle of the street. *Oh shit,* was all I could think as I ran over to him.

Like sharks in the water, those niggaz smelled blood and came out to eat. But a nigga gotta bring it to get it, and wasn't no way I was letting Boobie's li'l brother die on my watch.

Boom! Boom! Boom! Boom!

Boc! Boc! Boc! Boc! Boc! Boc!

I knocked the windows out of the car Butta was standing next to. I wanted to kill his fat ass so bad I could taste it. He retreated fast as a muthafucka! While Bleed stood next to Twin, covering him, I turned real quick to snatch him up, and that's when I noticed this crazy muthafucka shootin' from the sitting position. *This nigga is nutz,* I thought.

I pulled him up by his left arm while he was shootin' the whole time with the other. Then we heard the sirens coming and did what all real niggaz do: we ran, but to stop those cowards from hitting us in the backs, we kept bustin' at 'em over our shoulders.

"You hit?" I asked Twin when we got to his car.

"Naw, I'm good, dawg," he answered.

"A'ight meet up at the Mob quarters!" Then I jumped in the 'Rati and peeled out of the lot. When I got down the block, I looked through the rear-view mirror and saw the police pulling up on the scene. I exhaled, feeling better immediately. *Fuck, that was close!*

A couple of hours later we were back on that bullshit. We had met up, laid low, hopped in a G-ride, then got back to the triv. This was the type of shit we lived for. It wasn't nothin' wrong with Twin, either. That nigga just slipped on somethin' on the ground. *What the fuck?*

The shooting was all over the news and social media. Niggaz stay dry-snitchin' on Facebook. *I'm 'bout to give 'em somethin' to really talk about.*

"You ready to do this shit? Don't be acting like no li'l bitch when we get in there, either!" I turned around in the passenger seat, mimicking O-Dawg from *Menace to Society.*

"I'll beat yo' ass, Blood," Bleed shot back.

When I jumped out, the cold November air hit me straight in the face, forcing me to put my hoodie over my head. *Killin' season!* I knocked on the door at the trap house, then patiently waited. I had all day. Shit, it was one of my own spots.

"Speak yo' name or speak to death," a voice said from behind the door.

I looked at Bleed and Twin with a smirk on my face. I heard the unmistakable sound of an assault rifle being cocked and loaded. I yanked my hoodie off in frustration. "It's O-Dawg. Open the door," I demanded.

A few seconds passed, then the door opened and I walked in like I owned the bitch. I could tell we were the last muthafuckaz they expected to see. I stopped doing routine pop-ups years ago, so it was rare to catch me in the trap.

"What's Mobbin', Big O?" the nigga Flip asked me after placing the AK-47 back up against the wall.

I looked around, taking everything in. Nothing unusual. Chinese food boxes, video games, blunts, and a couple handguns. Then I looked at his sidekick, Major, who stuck his hand out, smiling like I was a fuckin' politician.

"I came to collect everything out the spot. We're shuttin' this one down," I cut straight to the chase.

He looked at me like I had two heads. "Oh. Burnside never said nothin' about that to me," he had the stupidity to say.

"Oh, so you work for Burnside now? This his shit now?" I growled at him.

"Naw, I didn't mean it like that," he backed down. "I just meant if Burnside would've told me, I could have had it ready for you." He was lying like a muthafucka.

"Well, I'm telling you now," I said with contempt.

He led me to the back room where all the money and work was at. I watched him closely as he stuffed the kilos and money into two duffle bags. I made sure to keep my eyez on the pistol poking out from his waist. I wasn't expecting no drama from him, but I wasn't about to underestimate him, either. A lot of suspect shit had already happened, plus Flip was a fool with that gunplay. The only problem for him was he was more loyal to Burnside than me.

When we got to the front room I cut straight to the chase. My gun was out and pointed at his head in the blink of an eye. "Convince me you ain't a part of the revolution," I said.

He dropped the bags, but didn't raise his hands in surrender, which was a bad sign to me. *He ready to die.*

Boc! Boc! Boc!

He dropped like a fly, dead to this world. He didn't move, spasm, shake, or none of that. He was wit' the reaper before he hit the ground. I crouched down and stared into his lifeless eyez for a few seconds. *He must've deserved it.* "I'm not convinced," I let him know, then closed his eyelids.

When I got up, Major had his hands in the air with Bleed poking him in the back of the head with his pistol. I sat down on the couch and stared through him. I was done playin' with niggaz. My best friend was dead.

"Convince me you ain't a part of the revolution against me," I demanded.

"O, I swear on my dead grandma, I don't know what you're talkin' about, my nigga! Ain't nobody told me nothin' about plottin' on you or none of that. I don't know what's going on!" he pleaded his case.

I stared through his soul and saw honesty. He really didn't know nothing or he deserved an Oscar, 'cause his life was on the line. There was only one problem with his truthfulness, though. "This was yo' main nigga, though, right? If somebody killed mines, I would ride hard for 'em," I said.

"Not if he went against the grain," he replied, tryna sound convincing. I wasn't, though.

"You ever read *Blood in My Eyez* by George Jackson?"

"Naw," he shook his head.

"Ask the Reaper to get you a copy."

Boom!

He dropped instantly, not knowing why he died. Bleed stood over him.

Boom! Boom! Overkill!

I grabbed the bags and got up outta there, leaving the door open. That would make it look more like a robbery.

We didn't say nothin' to each other as we cruised back to the spot. It wasn't shit to say. We were killin' our own men, and wasn't nothin' glorious about death. Wasn't nothin' glorious about the predicament we were in. This shit was life or death, kill or be killed. Flip was one of Burnside's main shooters. When it was time to crush his snake-ass, I didn't wanna have to look over my shoulder. I did what he should've did before he killed Boobie. I was a real war strategist, so I took this shit serious. I was ready to die about it. There was blood in my eyez.

Marcellus Allen

Chapter 6

Hearing my phone going off woke me outta my sleep a week later. I'd always been a light sleeper, but I was really on eggshells the past week. It was going down in the town, city under siege, fo' real! Niggaz were getting popped left and right nonstop. Burnside went ape-shit when Flip and Major's bodies were discovered. Everybody was out shootin' every hood. Most niggaz didn't even know why they were mad, they just wanted to ride.

"What's Mobbin'?" I answered for Burnside.

"Meet me at Applebee's by the Lloyd Center for lunch. We know who the rat is."

His words made me sit up. He had my full attention. "Who is it?" I demanded.

"Not on the phone, brody, but we got his bitch," he said.

I hung up with a smile on my face, and it's rare that I smile. I'd been tryna figure out who the snitch was since my lawyer first told me. Being so close to the truth had me so anxious and excited that my dick got hard.

I went searching for Olay. She still hadn't come off the pussy, but I was determined this morning. I didn't find her in the guest room or my son's room. I didn't smell no breakfast being cooked, so the kitchen was ruled out. *I know where she's at.* I made my way to the bathroom and knew she was in there as soon as I got to the door. I could smell all that expensive-ass lotion and body wash through the door.

I walked in while she was standing in the mirror lotioning herself up, butt-naked. "That pussy smell good. I'm tryna taste that," I had to let her know.

She turned toward me all surprised and shit, covering up her titties. "Get out, Marshawn," she demanded.

Yeah, right. I stepped all the way in, closing the door

behind me, and got right in her face. "I'm not about to keep playin' these games with you, Olay. You my bitch, so stop torturing me and let me hit that."

"I'm not your bitch, and I'm not letting you hit nothing," she crossed her arms and rolled her neck like all black women do. "You better go fuck that pregnant bitch you got." She just had to add that in.

I grabbed her and pushed her up against the door. I pressed my dick into her back while I growled in her ear. "Bitch, you 'bout to take this dick, and then I want you to go move all ya shit back in our room where it belongs."

"No, Marshawn! Get off of me!" she yelled.

I ignored her, dropped to my knees, and spread her cheeks. She stood on her tippy-toes when my tongue started lickin' her ass. She got to moaning and surrendered all fight shortly after that. I kept rotating between her ass and pussy, hittin' all the spots that drove her crazy. She poked her ass out a li'l more and watched me put this tongue on her through the mirror. We made eye contact through the glass for a split second, then it was back to the ass.

"I'm cummin'!" she screamed out.

I kept on sucking her pussy like it was the fountain of youth. Once I stuck my finger in her ass, she started cummin' and screaming at the same time. After I let her nut in my mouth, I slapped her ass and told her to bend over the counter. She bent over with no complaint. *I got my bitch back,* I thought as I slid up in her.

Thirty minutes later I was standing in the mirror zipping my Gape hoodie up over my bulletproof vest. *I'ma have to die in this muthafucka,* I decided right then and there. Teflon had probably saved my life two different times. I didn't even feel like the same nigga when I didn't have it on. I stared in the mirror at myself and what I had become. The hoodie matched the Air Max 97s on my feet. The jewelry was on point, as usual, and the blackness around my pupils told the story of my life, but the bags under my eyes told the world how tired and stressed I was.

"What's up, O?" Falon walked into my room all cheerful and shit.

Click! Click! I cocked the HK .40 Cal and stuffed it down the small of my back. "What's Mobbin'?" I faced her.

"I see you finally gave that bitch some dick. About time!" she laughed at her own joke.

"You know how I do. Now, what you want?" I still wasn't fuckin' with her ass. It was her fault Olay was trippin' on me. *Snitchin'-ass bitch.*

"Oh my God, Marshawn, you still mad about that baby shit? I told you I was sorry. I fucked up," she called herself apologizing.

"So, Joe yo' main nigga now, huh? Boobie dead, and you just jump on the next dick like he was nothin'?" I blasted her.

She sucked her teeth. "You know I loved that nigga! Don't make it sound like that. And I was messin' with Joe before he died, so don't come for me!" she raised her voice.

I looked her up and down with a look of disgust on my face. *Raspy bitch.* Then I walked out without speaking another word. Her ratchet-ass didn't deserve to communicate with real niggaz as far as I was concerned. *Why she even at my house?*

I pulled up an hour later at Applebee's with my nigga Meek Mill bumpin' through the speakers. That's who I bumped when I was in stunt mode, and I was definitely stuntin' on niggaz in the town. I couldn't be touched. I was untouchable. We in the middle of a war, and I stayed driving around in a bulletproof Maserati like *fuck dem pussies.* I knew niggaz woke up daydreaming about killin' me. *I'm hard to kill.*

I hopped out like a shark on land (more like floated) and shook Gotti up, who was parked next to me. I had called him and told him the triv cause I didn't trust these niggaz as far as I could see them. One thing I had to learn in this treacherous game was don't nothin' beat the cross but the double-cross.

"What's Mobbin'?" I gave my relative a gangsta hug.

"Shit, everything looks official. I think we just got lucky," he replied.

I nodded my head while looking up at the sky. It was one of those typical Portland weather days. The sky didn't know if it wanted to let the sun shine or drown us with rain, so we were stuck somewhere in between. I planned on making it rain, though.

We bumped into Beast and Premo by the front door. "What's Mobbin' with it?" I acknowledged them. They at least deserved that. They had put in major work since I had pressed the button. I'd seen their dirty work up close and personal. They were about that life.

"You already know, son. Holdin' shit down in case the crabs come through on some set-up shit," Beast spoke up.

The crabs? Set up? Fuck he talkin' about? I wondered as me and Gotti walked in the building. I was gon' ask Gotti, but figured I was about to get my answer.

"You know we gon' have to kill those niggaz just to be safe?" Gotti whispered.

I nodded my head at him. What's understood ain't gotta be explained.

Gotti led me to a table by the window, and as soon as I saw who the bitch was sittin' with Burnside and Joe, I instantly knew who the informant was.

"What's Mobbin' with y'all?" I shook them both up as I

took my seat. "How you doing, Felicia?" I smirked at her.

"Hi, O-Dawg," she said my name with contempt.

Bitch still mad I put her name in that song. She better fix her tone or I'ma slap her silly ass.

"A'ight, Blood, just give it to me raw, the short version. I'm sure just by seeing her here I already know what the triv is," I told Burnside.

I really didn't even like being in the presence of them snakes, but the situation was too critical to let my pride get in the way. *In due time,* I reminded myself and focused on the task at hand.

"Go ahead, baby," Burnside directed her.

"I walked in on my baby dad, Half Dead, talkin' to the detectives. He's been sneakin' out the bed in the mornings to go whisper on the phone in the front room. I got tired of it and started listening, thinkin' it was a bitch. Then I found out it was the two black detectives and he's an informant, and I heard him say y'all's name a lot on the phone about murders."

My heart dropped as I listened to her tell her truth. I knew she wasn't lying. I could feel it. Just hearing how this bitch-ass nigga was going out had my blood boiling. I was ready to purge somethin'. She said somethin' about a wire that really had my stomach turning.

"He doing what with a wire?" I needed clarification.

"He's been wearing it to all their gang meetings, recording everything they talk about," she repeated.

This some movie shit, Blood, I thought while shaking my head. "Does he know that you know?" I asked.

"Yeah. I confronted him as soon as he hung up. He knows how I feel about snitches since one is the reason why my dad is doing life," she replied.

Spoken like a real bitch. Too bad all these niggaz out

here didn't feel the same.

"What did he say?" I wanted to know.

"That he was doing it for me and his son. The gang task had planted some guns and drugs on him, and this was the only way out. He has to do it." Even she shook her head at his cowardice.

"You know how this is gon' end, right?" I stared into her eyes with the question. Her life depended on her body language.

"Yeah, I know, but the alternative is risking me and my son's life. Plus, I love Burnside, not him."

I nodded slowly at her answer. It wasn't often a female blasted her nigga for snitchin', let alone fed him to the wolves.

I pulled out a knot from my pocket and tried giving it to her.

"I don't need that. That's not why I'm doing this," she waved the money away.

I can respect that. "Felicia, your son is about to be without a father. I'm not disrespectin' you by offering you the bag, trust me on that. But trust me, you're going to need all the money you can for the future," I broke it down to her.

She thought on it for a second, then took the money with a *thank you* and an understanding smile. I smiled back at her, then made my exit with Gotti right behind me.

When I stepped outside, it was pouring down rain and God made thunder shoot through the sky. I didn't know if that was the truth or not, but I did know I'd given him a lot to be angry about. I knew my heart had turned into stone and there would be no redemption for my soul. I was past the point of saving, but I was okay with that. If God was examining my heart at that moment, he knew it was filled with hate. He knew this world was about to be short one snitch-nigga. It was also probably going to be short one real bitch. Not because she was foul or did anything wrong. I was done with leaving witnesses alive, and she was a witness. She also loved Burnside.

I ended up driving around the city on my solo trip for over an hour. I had Pusha T's *S.N.I.T.C.H.* on repeat while I debated with myself how to kill his rat-ass. That was the one thing in this dirty game no one could dodge: the snitches. Hell, even the snitches got snitched on nowadays. I knew how to minimize the shit when it came to those rat-fucks cooperating against us: kill them wherever we catch 'em, and make it brutal. But I knew this situation had to be handled with gloves. I had just the right nigga in mind.

I pulled on 45th and Killingsworth Street and parked in front of the green, one-level house that belonged to my li'l homie Juice. He came out before I could even park the car and jumped in.

I peeled off while letting the song play before I spoke my mind. "I got twenty bandz on the head of a snitch-nigga." I came out straight with it like it was normal plottin' a man's death. It had become normal.

"I kill snitches for free, anyways. Who the rat?" he spat, not giving a fuck.

That's why I fucked with his young ass, he was all action, no talk. He reminded everybody of his big brother, Big Juice. It was crazy. It was like my nigga, R.I.P., was still there and not in a casket. From his words, body language and gun game to even the chain around his neck, he was the exact replica of his brother. I'd been tryin' for years to bring li'l Juice into the family, but he wouldn't budge. His brother was a Blood from a different set, and they didn't ride for him hard enough for li'l Juice's satisfaction, so he refused to be a Blood and hated the Crips for killin' his brother. But he was mad loyal to me, and that's all that mattered at the end of the day.

"Half Dead. He on some real confidential informant shit right now. I need that handled ASAP. I'ma have his exact location and time sometime this week."

"A'ight, I got you," was his reply.

"I want you to send a message, too."

"I got you," he reiterated, then smirked at me.

Enough said. I kept driving in silence, deep in thought about all the shit the streetz was throwin' at me, but one thing was fo' sho: real niggaz always end up on top, so I knew I was gon' be coo' no mater what.

We pulled up to one of my trap spots and parked right in front of the house. The rain had slowed down some, but not enough to have the fiends waiting in line by the dozens. Phatz came out a minute later, runnin' toward my window. I rolled it down. "I need you to bring me twenty bandz out the safe real quick," I told him.

"A'ight, big homie." Then he ran back inside.

"Yo, O, I'm really feelin' this Maserati, my nigga. You killin' shit with this one," Juice spoke up.

"Wait 'til I cop that Bentley GTC on these hatin'-ass niggaz," I arrogantly replied.

We both laughed at the thought of that, then Phatz returned before he could respond. "This the twenty, right here." He handed me a shopping bag through the window.

"Good luck. I'ma come and holla at you and li'l Bobby in about an hour," I said while passing the bag to Juice.

I had been fuckin' with them two li'l niggaz heavy since I got outta jail. Ever since their situation, they had been on point and ridin' hard for the team. I was turning them into monsters I could use in the future.

I dropped by the studio and laid down a track called *No*

Mercy, then went and checked on Tamia.

"Fuck you, nigga! Get out!" she yelled as soon as I walked in.

She was sitting on the couch watching one of them fake-ass reality shows and eating a gallon of ice cream. I ignored her temper tantrum and sat down next to her.

"I love you, too, Tamia." I kissed her on the cheek.

"No, the fuck you don't, nigga." She put the ice cream down and faced me. "You clearly don't love your child 'cause you sho didn't come to the appointment for her yesterday. Punk-ass nigga!" she flashed on me.

Her? That's when it hit me. I was supposed to take her to the doctor so we could find out together what gender the baby was. *I fucked up.*

"Oh, shit!" I slapped myself on the forehead. "Why you didn't remind me, Tamia? You know I wanted to be there for that," I tried turning it around on her.

"Obviously you didn't or you would've remembered. Maybe if you wasn't over there crawling up that ho's ass you woulda been there for us!" she screamed, then broke out crying.

What kinda shit is this? I wondered, then pulled her in close to me. "I'm sorry, baby. I'll make it up." I shook my head at myself for forgetting somethin' so important.

"You can never make that up." She pushed me off of her, then wiped her eyes. "I'm done with this shit, Marshawn. I don't wanna be with you anymore. It's over. I can't keep playin' second to a bitch that's lesser than me. The same bitch that was going to let you rot in jail. I was coming to see you every weekend while she was in California. Probably gettin' some dick. You're never going to love me. I'm done," she spat while cryin' a river.

Each word was like a bullet to the chest, a dagger to the

heart. It hurt. I mean really hurt. She had some valid points, no doubt, but Olay was my everything, and I couldn't see myself without her. It just wasn't realistic. I never really understood how much Tamia was hurting until that moment. Until I looked in her eyez as she spoke those words. *What can I do?* I sat there questioning myself.

"Baby, you're hella emotional 'cause you're pregnant, and I understand that. I'm sorry about yesterday, I really am. I'ma leave so you can have time to think about what you really want," I told her, kissed her, then headed to the door.

When I turned around, she was back eating her ice cream like nothin' ever happened. *Maybe she is done.*

Chapter 7

Two Weeks Later

It was a rare sunny afternoon, so me and the wife decided to get outta the house. The plan was to take her and my son shopping at the mall, then shake to the zoo. My li'l man loved to see the wild animals, so that's what we were going to do. But money don't never sleep or take no days off, so I still had to get it. Plus I still hadn't recuperated all that money I lost while doing that County bid.

"He needs to hurry up, damn," Olay complained from the passenger seat for the fourth time.

"Here he comes right now, chill out," I told her.

"I don't know why you gotta do this stuff while we're in the car, anyways," she kept complaining.

I ignored her ass and focused on the black Benz that was parking next to me, making sure nobody was following him. I hopped out and popped the trunk, grabbing the bag with the three kilos in it. I got in Troy's Benz, closed the door, and tossed the bag on his lap. "What's Mobbin'? That's three of the same thangs from last time," I told him.

He grabbed a bag from the back seat, then handed it to me. "Good lookin' out. The money all there, as usual," he replied, shaking my hand to seal the deal.

"What's understood ain't gotta be explained. Let me go take my bitch shoppin' before she starts flashing out here. Be safe, and holla at me when you ready."

"A'ight, triv," he said, shook me up, then I was out.

I tossed the money in the trunk, then took my family shoppin'. For over an hour I bought my son every shoe and video game he wanted. I had to make two trips back to the car before he was ready to sit his ass down at the food court and eat his ice cream.

"You a bad li'l nigga," I told my son while I brushed over his waves with my hand.

"Uh-uh." He shook his head while licking his ice cream.

"And spoiled, too," Olay added, then started lickin' his ice cream, too.

He pulled his cone from her with an attitude and scrunched his face up. "Uh-uh! You spoiled, Mommy. That's why you eatin' my ice cream and not yours." He was dead-ass serious, too.

We looked at each other, then back at Mar-Mar and busted out laughing. He really called himself, checkin' his mama. The shit was epic. Olay kissed him on the forehead and apologized for the sake of peace. He quickly forgot about it and went back to asking about the lions.

"C'mon, li'l boy, before I beat you up in here. Matter fact, I'ma throw you in there with the lions when we get there," I threatened him while scooping him up.

"Uh-uh, Daddy! I'ma throw you in there and I'ma beat the lions up!" Then he ice cream-slapped a real nigga.

I put him down right when we got to the exit doors so he could hold hands with his mama, plus I had bags in my hands, and his li'l ass was getting heavier by the day. Soon as I stepped outside, I saw a group of four young niggaz walking my direction that put me on alert. *Fuck is these niggaz?* I touched my .40 outta habit and to make sure I was on point.

I don't know what it is about real street niggaz, but we can always spot a foe from a mile away. After being a part of so many gang wars, I had developed a sixth sense for the bullshit. My sixth sense was tellin' me to pop these niggaz. I could feel the negative energy radiating from the group as we got closer to each other. The looks on their faces gave them away. I yanked out and let the burner hang by my leg.

"You lucky you with yo' son, cuz, or we would air you out right now for Gucci Ty," a li'l short, ugly muthafucka had the audacity to say.

He must be crazy, I thought as we kept walking to the car. My blood was past boiling. I was on fire! I couldn't believe the fuck-nigga had the nerve to speak ill in front of my family like I was a bitch or somethin'.

Olay looked at me, pleading with her eyez. I bit my bottom lip and tasted blood. She hurried up and threw my son in the car and hopped in. I looked at the group, they were still muggin' me.

I put one finger in the air, signaling for them to wait one minute. I opened the door. "Get in the driver's seat and start the car," I told Olay.

"No, Marshawn! Get in the car! Let it go, please!" she begged me.

I didn't even think about no shit like that. They had violated me, and that was punishable by death in the streetz.

I backed outta the car and came up firing, no talkin'! *Take a deep breath. I know what I'm doing.*
Boom! Boom! Boom! Boom! Boom!
Two of them ran inside the mall, one across the lot, and the one with the big mouth had the heart to draw down.
Boc! Boc! Boc!
Boom! Boom! Boom! Boom! Boom!
I was walking up, shooting. He was walking backward. I wasn't duckin', hiding behind cars, or none of that shit. I was ready to die about it. I was on some emotional shit. Last time a pussy tried me while I was with my bitch, she got grazed in the head. I was past the point of giving out passes. When an enemy see me, he better eat, 'cause I'm tryna eat somethin'! Kill or be killed.

Boom! Boom! Boom!
My bullets struck the glass windows as the dummy backed into it. He ducked at the right moment or his forehead would have been missing. He turned around and opened the door while shooting blindly over his shoulder. I hit him in the leg as he escaped inside.
Boom! Boom! Boom!
I saw him hit the floor, then bounce back up, limping in the corridor. I thought about chasing him down, but quickly disregarded that plan. *Fuck that,* my common sense screamed at me.

I took off back to my car, hopping in the passenger's seat. My adrenaline was in overdrive. I leaned back and tried my best to block out Olay cussin' me out while my son was screaming his head off. It wasn't too hard. I just focused on what I was about to do to niggaz.

I still couldn't believe how dumb and untrained them young niggaz were. Their big homies should've taught them better. Should've taught them to show no mercy to a stone-cold killer of my caliber. I told myself at that moment that a message had to be sent. Respect and fear had to be reestablished by any means necessary. I was steady Mobbin'.

A few hours later I was pacing the dungeon floor with a heart full of hate and a mind set on revenge. Gotti, Twin, Burnside, Bleed, and Jersey Joe were standing there, just watching me. I had given them a play-by-play of what happened, and they were all ready to ride. We tossed ideas around, but none of them quenched my thirst until Gotti hit us with a bomb.

"I got word that Pressha's baby mama works at the bank on MLK," he told us outta nowhere.

"Which one?" I blurted out.

"Bank of America?" Bleed asked.

"Yeah, that one," Gotti nodded in agreement.

I looked at my watch. It was 6:30 p.m. *Too late.* But it was coo'. That just gave me more time to plan it out right. "We kidnappin' that bitch," I spat.

"That's what the fuck I'm talkin' about, son," Jersey Joe added, getting real excited.

"His baby mama is the white bitch, right?" I asked.

"Yeah, that one," Gotti answered.

"When we doing it?" Burnside wanted to know.

"Tomorrow, right when she gets off work. That give us enough time to do our homework. We 'bout to tap in on his Instagram and hers and get the drop on what car she drives and whatever else. The dumb bitch is white, so I'm sure she got everything on there. We 'bout to wake this nigga program up tomorrow," I said, already seeing the look on his face when he found out we got his bitch. That shit made me smile, somethin' I rarely did.

The next day came, and we were more than ready to execute our plan. We knew everything we needed to know. The shit was easier than expected. I guess he felt like he couldn't be touched. *I'm about to hit this nigga where it hurts.*

I looked at my watch for the fourth time. 5:10 p.m. The bank closed at five o'clock. We were expecting her at any moment. Me and Gotti were parked in the lot sitting in a stolen car, just waiting on her ass. The rest of the squad was camped out across the street in a stolen van. We went over every detail a hundred times. We knew what to do.

"There she go, Blood," Gotti pointed her out, getting hyped up.

I stared at her to get a good read on her. *Yeah, that's her,*

I thought as I started the car up. I watched her with hate as she made her way to her green Lexus. Soon as she started up, I drove out in front of her as planned. I looked in the rear view and saw the van pull up behind her.

"Let me know when she ready to turn," I instructed Gotti.

"I got you," he said while giving his eyez to the mirror.

We drove down MLK for a few minutes, just waiting for her to turn. It had to be like that 'cause wasn't no way we were kidnappin' no white bitch on the busiest street in Portland. Especially in broad daylight! Fuck that!

"She hit the right blinker," Gotti finally said.

I hit mine, then got over to the turning lane just before she did. I looked behind me to make sure the van caught the light. They did. We turned right on Mallory Street, which was perfect for us. As soon as I got to the next corner, I hit the brakes hard all of a sudden. The sudden stop made her have to hit her brakes, which is what we wanted.

Joe, Twin, and Bleed jumped outta the van with their guns aimed at the white bitch. "Get out of the car, bitch!" Bleed yelled.

She screamed as Joe yanked her out, but got quiet after he slapped her silly. Him and Twin threw her in the van while Bleed hopped in the Lexus. We all drove out like nothin' happened. It took less than thirty seconds.

Burnside drove them to the dungeon while me and Gotti followed Bleed to a coo' spot to dump the car. We had pulled it off, and I couldn't wait to throw it in those bitch-niggaz' faces. This was the same nigga who had shot up my car with my bitch in it. He grazed her in the head, but I didn't plan on missing. I was gon' snatch the heart out of his soft-ass chest. I smirked.

When we made it to the spot twenty minutes later, they already had her in the basement, handcuffed behind her back.

They all smiled when we walked in.

"Job well done," I said while shakin' them all up.

"Bitch act like she don't know nothin'!" Burnside spat.

"They all do until that heater in they face," I spat, then walked to the middle of the room where she was at. Her eyes were pleading with me. I was sure if she kept searching deep enough, she would realize I was the devil. I had no soul, only pain and revenge. Losing Boobie really put a black spot on my soul. Nobody knew how much, but they were going to find out.

I knelt down in front of her, keeping eye contact the whole time. "Listen to me, Charlene, and listen to me real good. I'm the nigga who your baby dad always talks about. The one he wants dead. I want him dead, and you're going to help me."

She started shaking her head and tryna say somethin' but the duct tape was blocking it out.

"Hold up. I'ma let you speak in a minute. If you don't tell me everything I wanna know, I'm going to kill you. Then I'm going to find your son and baby dad and kill them, too. But if you tell me, I'll spare you and your son. That's the deal."

I pulled the tape off her mouth. She was ready to break. I could feel it. The tears were running down her face. What a predicament to be in. I felt not a trace of sympathy for her. Them Crabs didn't have no sympathy for my bitch when that bullet hit her head.

"Please, let me go. Please. He doesn't discuss his street business with me at all, I swear. I don't know who you are," she pleaded.

I exhaled my frustration. "Where do y'all live?" I asked.

"Please, just let me go," she shook her head and begged.

"Where do y'all live?" I tried again.

"I can't tell you," she said, surprising the hell outta me. I had to take a second to make sure I heard her right. I looked at my team to make sure they were hearing the shit.

Joe walked over and punched the shit out of her. She flew outta the chair. I put her ass right back in it. She started cryin' even harder, and her eye started swelling up.

"Cracker bitch! You gon' tell us what we wanna know or I'ma beat ya ass all night! Try me!" Joe screamed in her face.

She sniffed real hard, then stared at him with defiance. "I'm not telling you. He always told me that if somebody ever snatch me up and tell me to set him up, not to do it. Because then him, me, and the baby would be killed. I'm not doing it, so just kill me," she said with conviction.

Joe punched her outta the chair again. She hit the floor and didn't move. "White devil bitch! I'll kill yo' ass, in here talkin' all that hard shit! Ho!" he yelled outta frustration.

I put her back in the chair. Her lip was busted and dripping blood. She looked at us with contempt.

"C'mon, baby girl. We got all night to do this shit. You don't really wanna die for this nigga, do you? Think about your son," I tried a different approach with her.

"I am. That's why I'm not telling you. I'll die for my son. Wouldn't you?" she asked and stared right through me.

Wouldn't I? I asked myself, then quickly disregarded the question. *Of course I would,* I told myself, then saw her in a new light. She wasn't a street nigga tryna play Braveheart. She was only a mother doing what they do best: protecting their children. I could respect that to the highest degree.

"Yeah, I would definitely die for my son. You sure this is how you wanna do it? I promise I won't kill yo' kid," I tried again.

"I can't do it," she said.

That shit touched my cold heart.

"Yo, son, she sayin' that right now, but watch when we

torture the ho!" Joe spat with venom.

"Naw, Blood, I'ma respect her gangsta. Take the cuffs off of her. Burnside, bring her phone over," I demanded. Joe looked like he wanted to protest, but I gave him one of those looks that said not to fuck with me.

"Unlock the phone so we can Facetime the nigga," I told her.

She did as told, and a minute later Pressha's bitch-ass face appeared on the screen. "Charlene, where you at? I've been callin' you for the last hour! You was 'pose to been home!" he yelled as soon as he seen her.

"Baby, I'm sorry!" she sobbed to him. She broke down crying, not able to get any more words out.

"What the fuck! What's wrong with you? Why you cryin'?" The panic was all in his voice.

"They got me!" she yelled through her crying.

"Got you? What the fuck is wrong with your eye?" he yelled.

I snatched the phone. I had heard enough. "Hello? Yeah, it's the kidnappers again," I said, mimicking DJ Pooh off the movie *The Wash.* I had always wanted to do that to somebody.

His face went from confusion to anger to defeat all within five seconds. I was lovin' it way too much. He knew it was over for him. I had just crushed his heart.

"Name the price, cuz," he stated, way too calm for me.

"Y'all hear this nigga, Blood?" I said to my homies. "Y'all come say hi to our favorite Crab homie," I said, waving them over. They all mean-mugged the camera while I just smiled at him. I planned on milking the situation for as long as possible.

I focused the camera back on me. "Real shit, my nigga, you trained yo' bitch real good. She won't give you up, and that's rare these days, but you gon' have to train another one, 'cause this bitch is dead. You failed to protect yo' family, dawg," I rubbed it on real thick.

"She ain't gotta give me up, cuz! We can meet right now! Anywhere! Send y'all location and I'm coming, and that's on Crip! Fuck y'all slob-niggaz, meet up right now! Leave the women outta this, you fuckin' coward!" he yelled and pounded his chest like he was scaring somebody.

"Leave women outta this? Ain't you the same nigga that shot my bitch in the head?" I yelled back, getting in my feelings. I turned to Joe. "Kill that bitch," I gave the green light. I turned the phone toward his bitch. I wanted him to watch her die. I wanted the shit to haunt him in his nightmares every time he closed his eyez.

Joe put the gun to the side of her head. "Say goodbye to yo' Crab-ass baby dad," he told her.

"I love you, daddy," she said, then broke down.

"Hold up! Whatever y'all want!" he screamed.

Boom! Joe knocked her noodles out. We watched her slump to the ground in slow motion, then he stood over her for the fuck of it. *Boom! Boom!* Overkill!

I turned the camera to my face. "Kill yo'self so you can see her faster. Blame her body on them li'l niggaz at the mall," I said, then disconnected on him. *I bet his ho-ass cryin' right now,* I thought, then smiled to myself.

We all looked at each other, not knowing what to say or do next. We were still surprised how it all played out. The last thing any of us expected was for the white girl to go out like she did. I stole a quick glance at her body, then shook my head. *What a waste.*

"I'm 'bout to start fuckin' with White girls, Blood, on me," Bleed said outta nowhere.

"I was thinkin' the same thang," Gotti added. We all

broke out laughing like that was the funniest shit we'd ever heard. Somethin' was wrong with us in the head, fo' sho.

"C'mon, let's clean this shit up and get ready for the get-back," I said, getting back into beast mode.

Marcellus Allen

Chapter 8

The next day I just chilled at Tamia's house and had her helping me count money. She had finally got off her trip and came to the realization she couldn't function without me, which was coo' with me 'cause I needed my rider bitch by my side.

After I dicked her down and made a few promises, we sat in the front room counting money for hours. Since I had been out, I hadn't counted none of my profits until that day. I would just drop the money off in the spare bedroom and get back to grindin' or ridin', whichever one the day called for, but today was the day I decided to count the bag.

"Tamia, is you gon' wrap that stack up or just let it sit there all day?" I asked her, full of frustration. The money machine she was using had been done counting the last stack, and it was just sitting there. It felt like it was over five minutes it had been done. She was so busy on her damn tablet online shoppin' that she didn't notice it. She'd rather be spending all the money instead of helping me count it.

She flipped me off. "Me and your daughter is tired," she had the nerve to say, then wrapped the money up and put another stack in.

"You ain't too tired to be online shoppin' and shit, spendin' all my loaf on heels and purses you ain't gon' ever wear and shit," I blasted her.

"Sure ain't," she said, then got right back on the computer like I ain't said nothing.

I shook my head, then looked around the front room. We had money either stacked up or lying around everywhere. We were over halfway done, but still had at least another hour of counting to do. I was tempted to call it quits, but I wanted to know exactly what my money was hittin' for. We had already counted a li'l over $300,000, so I was most definitely feelin' myself.

My phone going off snapped me outta my zone. "What's Mobbin', brody?" I picked up for Gotti.

"Hurry up and turn on the news! Shit just got real!" he yelled, sounding real excited about somethin'.

I jumped up and turned on the five o'clock news with high hopes of seeing one of my bitch-ass enemies dead on the screen. I smiled like a maniac when I heard what happened. *Bitch-ass nigga,* I thought as the reporter stood by the dead nigga'z car. What really touched my cold heart was when the lady explained how police had found a frozen rat on his lap. *That was genius. Why didn't I think of that?*

"O! Is you there, nigga?" Gotti brought me back to reality.

"Yeah, I'm here. Trust me, I'm here. Looks like he ain't Half Dead no more. He fully dead now. Snitch muthafucka," I growled with happiness.

"Them cross-towns gon' be sick now. They loved that rat," he laughed.

"Alright, I'ma tap in later. I'm countin' loaf right now. Tell the homies to be on point, though," I said, then hung up. I focused back on the news for a minute, listening to the bitch-ass gang task force lie to the public. I always found that shit funny.

"That's Half Dead that got killed?" Tamia asked.

"Yeah, that's his bitch-ass," I answered, then turned the TV off.

"Good, with his snitchin' ass. He ain't have no business snitchin' on you, anyways. Fuckin' coward," she spat with venom.

I wasn't surprised at all by her words. That's just how she was. She wasn't hella soft-hearted like most women were.

She grew up fighting her crazy-ass brothers and selling rocks on the corner. She was a real hood bitch. Her top-of-the-line beauty just threw everybody off.

"You a gangsta bitch, baby," I said, kissing her on the lips.

"Only for you, daddy," she purred.

"You know they're going to try to use the baby against you one day to tell on me. That's how they always come," I laced her and also wanted to pick her brain.

"Then she gon' be raised by either yo' mom or mines, 'cause I ain't telling them crackers shit," she stated in all seriousness.

I could tell by the way she said it she meant it from the heart. I felt that shit, plus she wasn't raised like most women. Her whole household was on gangsta time. They had a no-snitch policy. Her own mama would disown her, and that was real shit.

"A lot of people talk that 'I'll never snitch' shit, but when them handcuffs come out, shit change real quick," I teased her.

She looked at me all crazy. "Nigga, miss me with that shit, fo' real. I ain't no snitch-bitch. You needa be lecturing that golf-playing bitch you got! You got me fucked up! Punk-ass nigga! You better stop fuckin' with me while I'm pregnant before I stab yo' dumb ass," she yelled, then tried to stand up.

I pulled her back down, laughing like a muthafucka. That Spanish blood in her veins be causing her to go from 0 to 100 real quick. "I'm just playing with you, baby. I know you one hunnid. I just like getting you worked up," I copped out.

"Well, stop before you catch me on a bad day and I mess around and pop yo' ass! I don't like –"

I cut her off when I stood up, whipped out, and stuffed

my dick in her mouth. I gripped her head and tilted it back. "You talk too much, bitch," I said while I started slow-pumping her mouth.

She didn't have nothin' else to say.

I ended up staying in the house with her for the rest of the day. We counted money, fucked, and planned our future out. My phone kept blowing up with the news about Half Dead, so much that I turned it off. Plus I knew Tamia would trip if I didn't give her my full 100% attention, so I did.

The next day my producer, Rugar, hit me up all excited about some new beats he had made and wanted me to hop on them. With all the drama that was poppin' off, I hadn't had the chance to sit down and write no raps. Niggaz was out here losing their lives, so music was the furthest thing from my mind. I was out searchin' for revenge, but my music was poppin' out in the streetz, and my fans were demanding more. Rugar kept me alive on the internet and underground market. I was bigger than I realized.

When I got to the studio, it was empty except for Rugar working hard on the keyboard, as usual. I wasn't trippin'. I preferred it that way.

"What's Mobbin'?" I shook him up.

"Making beats and making money, the story of my life," he responded.

"Shit, at least you ain't gotta worry about nobody tryna take yo' life."

"Might as well, 'cause every time one of y'all get killed, it's like I do, too. Y'all niggaz are like my brothers, man. Just 'cause I ain't out here bustin' my gun don't mean I don't hurt the same as y'all. That shit broke me down when Boobie got killed, my nigga. I'm just hoping we can blow you up with this music shit before you get killed, too," he said.

Hearing Boobie's name and how it affected him really made me feel some type of way. *Only if you knew the truth,* I thought to myself. It was a dirty game we were playing, and it seemed like the more money that was made, the more treacherous it got.

"I feel you, brody, but I ain't going nowhere. You know I'm hard to kill," I said, being arrogant while I dapped him up. "Fuck all this emotional shit, though. What's good with the beats?" I changed the topic on him.

Rugar was a good nigga by all accounts, but he didn't suffer from the curse of the game. His soul wasn't blemished like ours. He was hurting from the loses, but time would heal that. My soul was tarnished for life, and my eyez reflected the darkness. I was in this shit 'til the casket dropped. It was in me, not on me. It wasn't a lifestyle, it was my way of life.

I rolled up a few blunts and got high while he played a bunch of beats for me. We discussed concepts, hooks, and flow patterns for over twenty minutes until I heard the first beat I wanted to slay. Once I found it, I lay back on the couch, working on the hook in my head.

I wrote to the beat for, like, thirty minutes, finishing the hook, first verse, and a li'l of the second. I had to put the pen and pad down when the buzzer went off, letting us know somebody was at the front door. I saw who it was in the monitor and buzzed him in. A minute later Li'l Juice walked in and dapped me up.

"What's Mobbin'?" I greeted him.

"Killin' pussies and fuckin' their bitches after the funeral," he answered with his arrogance on display.

I smiled at 'im. Not because of what he said, but because of who it reminded me of. That's exactly some shit his brother would've said. "I hear that slick shit," I responded, then turned toward Rugar. "This my brody, Rugar. He my in-house producer. Rugar, this my li'l bro, Juice," I made the introductions.

After they dapped up, I led Juice to my office so we could talk in private. It wasn't that I didn't trust Rugar, but when it came to murder, the less he knew, the better. Plus it technically wasn't my body, even though if the truth ever got out, some cracker-ass jury would convict me all the same.

I leaned back in my chair and asked the question I wanted to know the most. "A frozen rat? Where the fuck you find somethin' like that?" I wanted to know.

He started laughing. "At the pet store. They sell them for people who own snakes, so I figured the coward was a snake and a rat. Why not get it?" he explained, then busted out laughing again.

"That shit was on a whole 'nother level. I got somethin' for you." I reached under the desk, pulling out a brown paper bag. "This yo' bonus for that frozen rat. You got the whole city shook with that one." I handed him the bag.

He looked inside. "This a whole thang?" he asked with a questioning look.

"Yeah, li'l nigga, and there's a whole lot more of those with yo' name on 'em soon as you stop playin' and join the Mob," I propositioned.

"Here you go again with this shit. You know how I feel about clicks and shit. Ya can't trust 'em. But anytime you need me, you know I'm here," he denied me with the same line as always.

This time what he said really hit home. Around that time I couldn't trust nobody. We went from a united front to playing a secret game of thrones. I felt where he was coming from. "I'ma get you one of these days," I told him.

"Yeah, I hear you. Fuck all of that, though. What's up with Falon, with her thick ass," he said.

"She a gold digger, Blood. Trust me, you don't want that bitch. C'mon, Blood, I gotta go record this song."

When we got back to the front, Rugar already had everything set up for me to record, so I walked straight into the booth to do my thang.

"Yo, I'ma do the hook later after I change a few lines. I'ma do the first verse right now, though," I said, then put the headphones on.

I waited for the beat to drop then went in.

When I die, bury me with my favorite gun on me.
Had to bust back, name a time you seen me run, homie.
Ho-niggaz wanna drag my name through the mud,
Baby K with the drum, I'm a half a million up.
Fuck what they talk, I'm the only thing they talk about,
Then they beg for mercy when we in they baby mama house.

In it to the last man, sell it 'til the las' gram,
Mob life, we push the line like a marching band.
Word in Northeast. It's 20 thou on me.
Broke niggaz, I got more than that right now on me.
Hard to kill, so these snitches take deals on me.
Out on bail, still do a drill, tell me that ain't real, homie.
My $100,000 lawyer keep tellin' me to slow it down,
But I make fifty thou every time my feet touch the ground.
That's why I just laugh at the rumors, nigga,
And cop the big face every time I see my jeweler, nigga.

I walked out and joined Juice on the couch while Rugar worked his magic on the computer. "That shit was dope," Juice complimented, handing me the blunt.

My phone went off before I could respond to him. I saw it was Spike calling and answered it. "What's Mobbin'?" I greeted 'im.

"Yo, Blood, I got you a meeting with Def Jam. We gon'

have it in a few weeks out there in LA," he told me.

"Def Jam? How you work that one?" I asked.

"I played some people your music that work there, and they fuckin' with you. They done heard all yo' shit and see yo' buzz on the net. They tryna sign you." He was more excited than I was.

"A'ight, good lookin', brody. I'm actually with Rugar working on somethin' right now," I said.

"Bet! Tap in with me later tonight when you get home. We got a lot to talk about."

"Alright, brody," I said, then hung up.

Juice and Rugar were staring at me, waiting to hear the news. They heard the words Def Jam and locked in on my conversation.

"Spike said Def Jam wanna have a sit-down with me," I said, nonchalant, shrugging my shoulders like it was nothin'.

Rugar jumped outta his chair, yelling and being real animated. "That's what the fuck I'm talking about! We 'bout to blow up, nigga!" he announced to the world.

I laughed to myself 'cause it was rare he acted out like that. He was always the calm and laid back one, but I guess when a nigga's hard work starts to pay off, that'll do it to him. Even Juice had a smile on his face and started giving me mad props.

They seemed more sparked than I was about the news. I felt good about the triv, but I wasn't about to hop up and start doing no jumping jacks. Wasn't nothin' official yet, they just wanted to talk. Plus I knew how those record labels got down. They were the biggest crooks and loan sharks in the water. If they thought they were about to pimp me out, then they had another thing coming. But I didn't wanna rain on nobody's parade, so I kept my feelings to myself.

We ended up calling all the homies and telling everybody

to meet up for the celebration. We were celebrating my future deal and the rat that was killed in his car. I had a lot to be happy about.

We all met up downtown at the Kit Kat strip club. It was one of the most poppin' clubs in the town, so we definitely had to make our appearance. The whole Mob was in there, about thirty deep, just to let the rest of the city remember who ran Portland. The last month had been real stressful, so we needed to release some tension. And what was better than big-booty strippers?

"Yo, you gotta start smiling around this bitch," I told Twin after I noticed he was the only one not having a good time. *Fuck wrong with him? I asked myself.*

"It's hard to smile when amongst the enemy," he growled, then gave Burnside the look of death.

I looked at Burnside having the time of his life with a bottle of Cîroc and two strippers poppin' their asses on him. He didn't have a care in the world.

"You gotta learn how to put your mask on, li'l bro, so when it's time to take it off, they'll never see it coming," I dropped a jewel on him.

"Fuck all that, dawg. I'm ready to murk somethin'. I'm tired of this 48 Laws of Power bullshit," he shot back.

"It's almost time. Trust me on this," I said, then pulled a stripper down on my lap. While she worked hard for her money, I looked around at my crew. Everybody was having a good time. From the outside looking in, we couldn't be closer than we were. We were on top, and from the way stuff was looking, we would never fail. But I knew better. I knew I was surrounded by snakes. *How many of them were in on it? I asked myself.*

"Yo, O?" Jersey Joe patted me on my shoulder, snapping me outta my thoughts. "This nigga over here talkin' 'bout he wanna holla at you, son," he nodded at two cats standing by the V.I.P. entrance.

I screwed my face up. "Fuck they want?" I asked, not recognizing either of them.

"Say they wanna talk business," he told me.

"The point of us being in V.I.P. is so we ain't gotta be bothered with the bottom feeders. Fuck it. Tell 'em c'mon so I can hurry up and dismiss them." Joe signaled for Premo and Beast to let the cats come to me while I told the stripper to come back later.

I knew the moment I saw how those two clowns walked I wasn't doing business with them. They whole swag was off. They were cops.

"What's up, O-Dawg? They call me Scarface," the dark-skinned, buff one stuck his hand out.

I shook it half-ass and asked, "Who is 'they'?"

"What you mean?" he asked, sounding confusing.

"You said 'they' call you Scarface, right? I wanna know who is 'they'? Where you from?" I broke down.

"Aw, I'm from Charlotte, North Carolina," he answered.

"Who is you? Manolo?" I asked his skinny-ass sidekick.

"Naw, I'm Shooter," he said, trying way too hard. I made eye contact with Bleed and Gotti, then everybody started closing in on them.

"Alright, what can I do for y'all?" I played their li'l game.

"We out here lookin' for a plug, and we heard you the man to come holla at," he said, then paused. When he realized I wasn't talking, he continued. "We wanna cop at least ten thangs," he said, leaning closer to me.

"Oh yeah?" I faked interest.

"Word," he said while smiling.

"At first I thought y'all two niggaz were on some

confidential informant type of shit. You know, the usual. Cowards getting caught up and deciding to set real niggaz up for the pigs. But now I got it all figured out. Y'all ain't no street niggaz turned snitch, y'all some house niggaz, born and raised."

"Naw, you got us fucked up," Scarface cut me off.

"Cop, please. They don't even say 'word' in North Carolina, for starters. I used to get money in Raleigh. Trust me, I know. Y'all whole presentation was wrong, especially that Scarface shit! A real nigga would've said 'face' or somethin'. Go tell gang task to suck my dick, and while you at it, go find out what happened to the last snitch," I said, then waved them away.

They didn't even try to put up a fight or nothin'. They just walked out with their heads down. I couldn't believe that shit. We all yelled, laughed, and taunted as they made their exit. *Fuckin' clowns,* I thought while I hit the bottle of Cîroc.

"You think that was local or the feds?" Gotti asked after everything went back to normal.

"The feds are way smarter than that. They would've used real street niggaz facing time to get at us. They definitely woulda used a Portland nigga, not no fake-ass out-of-towner. This shit got punk-ass gang task written all over it. There some fuckin' trucks, Blood," I theorized.

"I think they're desperate now that Half Dead is gone," he agreed with me.

"I think they're about to put the heat on us now," I concluded.

"We'll be ready, like always, for them," he said.

I nodded my understanding, then focused back on the scene around me.

I soon got mesmerized like everybody else in V.I.P. by watching Falon give Jersey Joe the best lap dance in the club.

The way her ass bouncing and poking out of her skirt had every nigga in there lusting. Including me. I had to hurry up and snatch up a stripper bitch to take my mind off my bitch's li'l sister.

The whole club was poppin' for the next twenty minutes until we saw a group of niggaz come storming the V.I.P. entrance. "Rollin'!" one of them yelled out.

I tossed the stripper off me just as they got past the ropes. I smirked at the group once I recognized the men approaching us. *About time,* I thought as I crossed my arms, waiting on them to walk over. My adrenaline got to pumping as I waited for the inevitable to happen. All my homies were up and anxious for battle. The whole club had their eyez locked on us.

"What's rollin' with you niggaz, cuz?" Big Lurch said once they were in speaking distance, disrespecting us.

"What's brackin', Blood?" Burnside shot back, getting right in their faces.

I stood there with my arms still folded, muggin' their whole squad down. It was about twenty of them in total, and they looked like they were ready to wreck some shit.

"What's up with that disrespectful shit you said on that song about us?" Big Lurch aimed his question at me.

"The friends of my enemies are my enemies, too. Y'all fuck with them Gutta Squad niggaz real tough, so it's fuck y'all, too," I broke it down for him like a math problem.

"So, that's what it is?" he needed clarification.

"That's what it is, Blood." I didn't budge.

Soon as the words left my mouth, he punched me in it, knocking me down on the couch. By the time I jumped up, it was a full-fledged riot poppin' off. Everybody was in there, throwing blows. I picked up a Cîroc and smashed it over the head of some nigga that was fighting with Twin. We stomped him out for a second, then I moved on, looking for Lurch's bitch-ass. I saw him and Jersey Joe going blow-for-blow in the corner of the room. I grabbed my waist momentarily, forgetting there wasn't no gun there. Ain't nobody getting in the Kit Kat with no pistol. I snuck up on 'im and wrapped him up in the *choke 'em, no smoke 'em*!

"Time to go to sleep, Crab," I growled in his ear, then put the pressure on him. He started bucking real wild to get free, but he wasn't getting out of it. I had his ass in the death grip.

Joe went East Coast on a nigga and spit a razor out of his mouth and got to slicing him up. Lurch went berserk tryna get free from that razor, but I held on. I was determined to make him pay for takin' off on me like I was some regular nigga.

Crack! Somebody busted a bottle over my head, forcing me to let Lurch go. I stumbled a few steps, tryna gain my balance back. When I did, it was a bitch standing in front of me with a broken bottle in her hand. She was acting like she was gon' stab me with it.

Pow! Pow! I hit that ho with a two-piece, dropping her dumb ass to the ground, then kicked her for disrespecting a real nigga.

Security rushed in hella deep, holding tasers and shit. *Oh, hell naw!* "I'm telling y'all right now, Blood, if one of y'all touch me with a taser, I'm coming back shootin'. I'm big O-Dawg from the Mob. Check my résumé," I threatened them.

"Get the fuck out, right now! Everybody!" the biggest one yelled.

I felt my eye start to burn out of nowhere. I rubbed it and the side of my face, then stared at my hand. My anger rose 100 degrees. I had blood in my eyez.

I mugged them Crips and let 'em know what time it was. "We going to the pistols now, and that's on Boobie!" I yelled while pointing my fingers in a gun motion.

"Nigga, fuck Boobie and slobs!" one of the Crips yelled out.

Twin flew over there and dropped the one that said it. Next thing I know, we right back to scrappin' in that muthafucka! We didn't stop until somebody yelled that the real police were outside. That's when we blew that joint, but not before one of those house niggaz tased me. Bleed snuffed 'im to the ground, then we kicked 'im a few times. We got up outta there, but not before I added his face to my mental rolodex. Now he was on my kill list. *I warned him.*

Everybody hit the parking lot and scattered like roaches. I had to check in the hospital for the big-ass cut that had swole up on my head. It was poking out like one of those cartoon characters and bleeding everywhere! I had to get six staples in my head, then got discharged. I was mad as a muthafucka, but like my man Nas said, *"I got stitched up and left the hospital the same night."*

When I finally made it home around 4 o'clock in the morning, Olay was wide awake on the couch, just anxious to cuss me out. I seen it all in her face. She was hot!

"Baby, look what them bitch-ass niggaz did!" I got pumped up, bending over and pointing at my head.

"Oh my God! What happened?" she freaked out.

Yeah, I know how to get yo' ass, I thought while I exaggerated my injury. She forgot how mad she was and started catering to my needs. I smiled.

Chapter 9

I woke up the next day with a massive headache and Olay shaking me, talking about the police was outside. *What the fuck?* Hearing the words no real nigga ever wanted to hear, especially a D-boy, had me jumping from under the covers in record-breaking time. I ran to my security monitors and saw it was only two cars stuck at my gate. A gang task detective car and a white Camry. *This can't be no arrest or search warrant with only two cars,* I thought.

"Did you talk to them?" I asked.

"Yeah, on the intercom. He said they had a court order for ankle monitoring," she told me.

I picked up my cell phone and hit my lawyer's private line. "The police at my gate talkin' about a court order," I said before he could even get a word in.

"That's correct, Mr. Anderson, and I've been calling you all morning about it. They got the judge to put you on ankle monitoring for thirty days. Their informant was killed, and they're claiming the spark in gun violence is due to your release on the streets," he informed me.

"I'll be at your office later on," I said, then hung up. I was pissed off.

"Go let the pigs in while I tighten up," I instructed Olay.

I made them pigs wait outside for ten minutes before I opened up the door with a blunt in my mouth. The frustration and contempt was written all over those house niggaz' faces.

"What the fuck y'all want? 'Cause I know they didn't send just y'all three to come arrest me. When it's my time to go, I plan on bangin' it out with the National Guard," I spat, full of arrogance.

It was Detectives Rogers and Freeman, along with some old-ass cracker that looked like a probation officer. I blew the weed in the air right in their pig-ass faces. I knew I was getting under their skin, standing in a Prada robe in the doorway of a mini mansion with no care in the world. I seen it in their eyez.

"First off, we're not here to arrest you, scumbag," Detective Rogers said while handing me some court documents. "We're here to put you on G.P.S. Monitoring for thirty days and make sure you understand the rules," he explained.

I already knew all this, but still decided to stand there reading the paper to fuck with them. After I was done fake-reading it, I blew some smoke in the air.

"Alright, let's get this shit out the way, 'cause I got money to make," I said, then walked in the house.

"Don't you think you should put that weed out until we leave? We are a part of law enforcement, you know?" the fake probation officer said.

I sat down on the couch and blew some more clouds into the air before responding. "Cracker, you in my muthafuckin' mansion. You're the uninvited guest, not me. The last time I checked, smoking weed in Oregon was legal, especially in the house, so fuck what you talkin' about and do ya job so y'all pigs can get the fuck out," I blasted his ass.

His face turned red while he bit his cheeks in frustration. He looked at the house niggaz who were too busy staring at me, making sure I understood their level of hate.

I'ma kill one of y'all before it's over and done with, I thought while I stared them back down.

"You know we're going to win at the end of the day? You do know that, right?" Detective Freeman said.

"I guess my books gon' be at the maximum, then, just like my nigga Big Meech. I'll live better in prison than you three punks could ever hope to on the streetz. I'm untouchable, race traitor," I shot back.

"Can we get this over with now?" monitor man spoke up.

I laughed at their pathetic asses while I put my right leg on the table. "Put it on my right ankle. Ya dealing with a real Blood," I demanded.

He didn't hesitate to hurry up and put the stupid black box on me so he could get up outta there. I loved to make the white man uncomfortable and did so any chance I got.

"You know why we're doing this, right?" Detective Rogers asked.

I looked at him like he was dumb. "According to your document, your informant was killed. Y'all believe I did it and I'm somethin' like a black Al Capone. Does that sound right?" I taunted them.

"We know you had Half Dead killed, and we're going to get you for that, but what made it personal was when y'all killed Charlene Davis for no reason. She was an innocent woman, you piece of shit. I'm personally going to make sure you get the death penalty for that," he threatened.

"So you're mad about the white woman? That figures since you are an Uncle Tom, but as of right now I'm exercising my right to not speak without my attorney," I said further pissing them off.

We mugged each other until the monitor was done being shackled to my ankle. I found it quite amusing, though. I knew them punks really didn't want no green room action with me, like the nigga Consequence from *Love & Hip Hop* said. They just felt like acting tough in front of the white man, but shit like that was the reason why people's mamas be cryin' at the funerals.

When it was time to kick them out, I stood on my steps and looked those pussies right in the face. "When my thirty days are up, I'ma make sure y'all gon' have to work overtime. Y'all just fucked up," I threatened them.

They nodded at me and left. I went straight to the couch and called my brother Jaxx, telling him to come over ASAP. I was mad as fuck about being on the ankle monitor. It was really gon' put my movement on a standstill, I could feel it!

I put the news on while I waited for my brother to get there. What I saw made me smile and caused my stomach to drop at the same time. I turned the TV up and pressed record.

Thirty minutes later, me and Jaxx had just finished watching the news segment for the second time together. I knew shit was about to get real, but I still wanted to hear my big brother's opinion. "What you think, bro?" I asked.

"Y'all niggaz going to jail this time, fo 'sho! They just said the coward Half Dead was a D.E.A. informant and was assassinated because his cover was blown. They said a rat was found on his lap and he was scheduled to testify against you. Yo' ass going to jail, and you ain't welcome to my house no mo', either!" he said, then started laughing at me.

This nigga always thinks shit funny. I should fire on his ass, I told myself. I didn't feel like even being around that clown no more at that point. I was feeling the walls start to close in on me, and all he could do was laugh?

"I'ma have Gotti handle all the shipments from now on until I cool down," I told him, then walked away to my room. *Fuck Jaxx!*

"They gon' cool yo' ass down in that cell!" he yelled at my back.

When I made it to the bedroom, Olay was sitting on the edge of the bed, cryin' like a muthafucka. It always broke my heart to watch her cry. I felt like she was too pure and innocent and beautiful to cry. I turned off the TV she had obviously been watching and kneeled in front of her.

"Baby, stop cryin', please. You know them white people

just love to hear themselves talk. There's nothin' to worry about," I tried to soothe her.

"Oh yeah?" she sniffed and wiped her eyes. "Then why did you call your brother over here, then? Why is your eyes saying your soul is worried? Stop tryin' to lie to me, 'cause I'm not stupid, and you know that, Marshawn!" she shot back.

Damn, she got me, I thought to myself. "Of course I'm a li'l shaken up by it, but at the end of the day I'm Gucci. You know I'm too smart for them crackers, baby." My arrogance was coming back.

"I'm not talkin' about jail, Marshawn. I'm scared they're going to kill you or have you killed," she sobbed.

That's the least of my worries. "Baby, niggaz been tryna kill me since I was 14. You know that. I'm not going in that casket until I'm old and gray, and I'm willing to kill whoever I have to in order to keep the blood flowing through my body. You, out of all people, should know by now I'm hard to kill. Fuck these niggaz!" I spat as I rose to my feet.

Hearing myself speak the truth was getting me pumped up. Shit, I wasn't worried about nobody coming for my head. That's what the Russians made AKs for.

"It's different now, and you know it. Now you're on top, and them people know they gotta kill you in order to get you out the way. You're going too hard on them, baby. You've gotta slow down," she lectured me.

I shook my head. "I can't slow down right now, baby. It's too much standing in my way."

"You killed that innocent woman, Marshawn! Was she in your way, too? And don't deny it, 'cause it's been all on Facebook. You went overboard with that, and she's white! Now y'all killed the informant! You're doing too much, and it's scaring me! Okay?" she yelled, then broke down cryin' again.

I don't gotta go through this shit with Tamia, I thought as I slowly inhaled, then exhaled. "I didn't see everybody cryin' over you when that bullet grazed yo' head," I hissed, then lifted her chin up so she stared directly in my eyez. "I'm not going too hard, baby girl. If anything, I'm not going hard enough on these fuck-boyz. But don't you worry about being scared, 'cause soon as this monitor comes off, I'ma finish my breakfast. Anybody that's my enemy is going into the ground. Then you'll feel safe again."

I kissed her on the forehead, then walked out. I was done talking, plus I had a whole lot of shit to set in order for the next thirty days. The pigs really thought they were doing somethin' by putting me on G.P.S. Them punks must have forgotten I didn't have to be around to make shit hot! I was about to remind them.

The next day I woke up early and got the hell up out the house. Olay was still on her li'l trip, but I knew she'd get over it in due time. I bounced to Tamia's spot and dicked her down, then let her slide with me to the studio. She was always complaining about me not taking her nowhere with me since I'd been outta jail, so I decided to let her tag along. Plus my Mob niggaz loved her.

"Blood, that video you put on Snapchat with the house niggaz is funny as fuck!" Bleed laughed from the couch directly across from me.

I had put the whole footage of the house niggaz talkin' that high-power shit in my front room. Them idiots didn't even realize I had cameras throughout my crib. The last 24 hours on social media had been nothin' but comments about that video and clips from the news about Half Dead being a rat. The shit was pure comedy.

110

"I know they sick right now, but they really gon' be sick when I get off this bracelet," I replied.

"Have you read what those squad niggaz been sayin'?" he asked with disgust.

"Naw, I ain't had time yet. What's up?"

"They on there talkin' 'bout Half Dead ain't no rat and we are salting his name. Talkin' 'bout where the paperwork at? That video is all the paperwork they need," he told me.

"You know how it go down here. Everybody fucks with snitches as long as they don't tell on them. Typical Portland shit," I shot back. I wasn't surprised at all by what he said. That was what the game had turned into, and it was only getting worse. Oh well. As long as my team stayed snitch-free, that's all I cared about.

"Yo, Tamia? Yo ass is getting fat! I mean that both ways!" Gotti said when Tamia stood up to go to the bathroom. We all started laughing.

"Fuck you, nigga!" she said, then punched him before walking off.

"I'm still surprised Olay ain't killed you in yo' sleep," Gotti said.

"She knows she can't live without me, Blood. Anyway, I forgot to tell y'all that Def Jam holla'd at Spike, and they wanna have a sit-down with me," I told everybody.

"Nigga, what? We 'bout to be on fo' real now," Bleed got all excited.

"We already on. We self-made, and don't never forget that. And I'ma make sure I tell them crackers that when I meet up with them, too."

"When the meeting?" Gotti asked.

Fuck, I forgot to tell Spike I can't fly to L.A. now. "I don't know now, since I can't leave the state. It was supposed to be in a few weeks," I spat angrily, getting mad all over again at the house niggaz.

"We gon' kill dem fuck-niggaz, dawg, 'cause that's all I care about," Twin finally said somethin'. He took a sip of his lean while staring me dead in the eyez. I could feel the hate radiating from his body.

He starting to think I don't care no more, I thought as I stared back into his pitch-black, unforgiving eyez. "I promise you, li'l bro, the moment this monitor comes off, we cleaning house. We purgin' on anybody that ain't family," I told him.

"I'ma hold you to that, dawg," he replied with a hint of attitude.

Was that a threat? I wondered.

"I got a plan for –" I stopped when Tamia came back and sat down. I trusted Tamia with my life, and she was definitely a part of the team, but I still didn't feel comfortable discussing future murders with her, especially the shit I had planned. We were gon' put pressure on the Portland Police Department.

"Yo, Rug, you ready for me yet?" I asked, knowing damn well he been ready.

"Yeah, c'mon," he answered.

I gave Tamia a kiss and told my goons not to try and get at my bitch while I was gone. I stepped in the booth and got in my zone. The song I wrote the night before was called *Hard 2 Kill,* and that's exactly how I felt. The beat dropped, and I went in.

Snitches get killed, they homies still praise 'em,

Laughin' while they fakin', I'm ready to die like Jamaicans,

But I'm hard to kill, so y'all better put up a half a mil.

Everything on the Maserati is bulletproof, pussy, even the grill,

So fuck every dead nigga that the Mob done killed.

Put me in the cell with Big Meech, 'cause I Mobz fo' real.
The beat cut off outta nowhere, killin' my vibe. I looked up from my phone and saw everybody standing up looking at me. Gotti waved me over. *What the fuck?* I thought while I walked out of the booth. I could tell from their facial expressions that this wasn't no good news, but when I locked eyez with Gotti and seen the sorrow, I knew somebody died.

"What's the triv? Who died?" I walked up and got straight to the point. *Please, God, don't let it be Olay or my son,* I prayed to myself.

"It's Li'l Bobby," Gotti said, then shook his head. "They got the pictures all on the net. They hit 'im with the bitch shit," he told me, then passed his phone.

What I saw made my heart drop, then quickly filled it up with anger. They had my li'l nigga laid out on the steps to some house. The way he was stretched out in those awkward-ass positions was somethin' I'd never forget. I could easily see the AK shells on the ground that matches the bitch-ass holes in his body. Then they had the nerve to take a picture and post it?

"Whose page is this on?" I growled, barely recognizing my own voice. *They did my li'l nigga dirty,* was all I kept thinking.

"It's on Pull-Out's page, and Pressha's, too. They been talkin' hella shit about it. Posting Mozzy lyrics and shit," he spat with venom.

I gave his phone back. "This just happened?" I asked.

"Yeah, it's fresh. The location is off of 15th and Freemont," he said.

I gave Tamia the keys to the 'Rati. "I'll call you when I'm ready," I said, then looked at my niggaz. "C'mon, we going over there right now," I demanded.

They all started gathering their shit without any words

being spoken. What was there to say, anyway?

Tamia hugged me real tight, then put my hand on her stomach right before I got to the door. "I will never tell you not to handle your business, daddy. Just keep in mind that you have on that monitor, and we have a baby on the way," she pleaded, then gave him a deep kiss.

This a real bitch, I thought as I nodded, then stepped outside into the cold air.

***

Two days later

I pulled up in the 'Ville and parked right across the street from Li'l Bobby's mother's house. I sat there for over five minutes staring out the window, looking at all of the distraught faces in mourning. The snow hadn't started to fall down yet and the weather wasn't at freezing temperatures, so people were standing outside, probably tryna escape the sorrow that was no doubt filling the air up inside the house. I watched a few people look in my direction, and some even pointed at my car, then started to talk amongst themselves. I couldn't go nowhere without standing out. *The price of fame.*

"You ready, Blood?" Bleed asked, tired of just sitting there.

"Can anybody ever be ready to talk to a dead man's mother?" I asked him back. I opened the door, not waiting on him to reply. There was nothin' he could say, and the question was more directed at my soul than him, anyways. I gripped the cold steel as the wind attacked my face and sent chills through my body. I didn't even try to fight the coldness. My body and soul were used to it.

When we got inside, Burnside, Gotti, Twin, and Jersey

Joe were already in there, mingling with Li'l Bobby's family and friends. Everybody had a plate in their hands and the air smelled of food, but the grief could be felt. I didn't want no food, though. I wanted to purge. I shook my niggaz up, then stood in the corner, taking everybody in.

"Do you want me to make you a plate?" Rita came over and asked me. She was Li'l Bobby's older sister and a female I used to mess around with a li'l bit. Even though she was hurt and it was obvious she'd been cryin', she still looked beautiful. I had to remind myself where I was and what I came to do.

"Naw, I'm Gucci. Thank you, though. I do wanna holla at your mama, though, whenever she feels comfortable," I told her.

She nodded in understanding. "She's in the back room with Phatz right now, tryna lecture him. Come on, let's go save him," she said, then smiled. Probably her first in days.

Rita knocked on the bedroom door first, then opened it without waiting for a response. "It's me, Mama," she announced herself, then added, "Somebody wants to talk to you."

I walked in not knowing what to expect, but fully prepared to take whatever was thrown at me. I had been around so many grieving mothers in my life, and on more than one occasion I'd been treated like I was the devil himself. Like I had killed their child.

What I saw was Phatz sitting on the edge of the bed, looking like he didn't know if he was ready to kill or if he wanted to cry. Li'l Bobby's mother was standing over him, and it was clear we interrupted her lecture. Once Phatz realized it was me in the room, his whole demeanor changed, then he hopped off the bed with a whole new attitude.

"Mama, this is Marshawn. Him and Bobby were real

close," Rita introduced me. She laid it on thick, though. Bobby was my li'l goon, but we weren't that close. We had actually just started bonding since I got outta jail.

"Hello, Ms. Wallace. I'm sorry for your loss. He was like a li'l brother to me." I laid it on thick myself.

She stared at me for a few seconds, and it felt like she was peaking at my soul. I watched every emotion ripple through her eyez one at a time. Pain, anger, confusion, hate, sorrow, contempt, and then finally love. "I know who you are. My son talked about you a lot. You were his idol," she said with a painful smile.

Idol? I never knew he felt like that. I ain't no damn idol, I said to myself.

"Plus, I've been seeing you on TV, too, O-Dawg."

"Those are lies," I lied my damn self.

She shook her head. "I doubt that very seriously for some reason. I'm no dummy. I know what y'all out there doing in the streets. I know what my son did," she said, trying not to choke up.

"We don't be doing nothin', Mama Wallace," Phatz jumped in, still tryna plead his case.

"Boy, shut up before I get mad. I'm tryna keep you outta prison," she flashed on him.

"Prison?" I asked without thinking.

"Where he's headed if he don't stop runnin' around here shootin' at people over my dead son. I just lost one, and I don't wanna lose another one," she explained.

She had a point, and I felt where she was coming from as a mother. But I wasn't a mother. I was a killer. "I came over to give you this, Ms. Wallace," I told her, then pulled a big envelope from outta my jacket. She took it and opened it up real slow, then looked at me with questioning eyez. "It's to pay for the funeral and whatever else. If you ever need help with anything else, please get in contact with me," I said with sincerity.

"Thank you very much." She hugged me tight. I could feel the love coming from her. It touched me deep inside my heart and made me feel a way I hadn't felt in a long time. Her love and heartache made me wanna cry for some strange reason. It set my soul on fire!

"Will you keep him safe? 'Cause Lord knows he ain't gonna let it go," she asked after finally letting me go.

I looked at Phatz. "I'm not, either, Ms. Wallace. But I'll do my best to keep him alive." I kept it trill with her.

She nodded her understanding to me, then I walked outta the room. There wasn't nothin' else that needed to be said, and that was one of the hardest things I had to do. *I'm glad that's over,* I thought as soon as my feet touched the hallway floor.

"How much money was that?" Phatz asked me.

"Not enough to bring her son back," I dropped a jewel on him.

We stayed over there with his family for another hour, then it was time to shake. Being in the house with all those sad people had really taken a toll on me. I hugged my niggaz' mama one more time, then allowed Rita to walk me to the car. She had been hinting at us spending some time together, but I wasn't with it. Even though she had been my bitch years ago, I still felt foul for even thinking about fuckin' the dead homie's sister.

"Are you going to call me, O?" We were all posted up outside, tryna figure out what to do next when she asked.

I was about to blow her off, when Bleed yelled out, "Ain't that them niggaz?"

I didn't hesitate one second. I pushed Rita to the ground and yanked out.

"Squad!" somebody yelled right before the shots.
Boom! Boom! Boom! Boom! Boom!
Boc! Boc! Boc! Boc! Boc! Boc!
Boom! Boom! Boom!
Them niggaz was on us somethin' serious! I hit the ground like any real nigga would do when that many shots were going off. That's when I saw who it was that was bustin' like that. Butta, Pressha, and Pull Out were walking down the street, tearing us off. I held my .40 with two hands and aimed right at 'em.
Boom! Boom! Boom! Boom!
Boc! Boc! Boc!
At that point, everybody started shootin' at one time. I knew we had them out-gunned and their element of surprise was over. I jumped up, still firing, and got behind a car for cover. They were at least still fifty feet away, standing in the street, gunnin' at us.
Boom! Boom! Boom! Boom!
Boc! Boc! Boc!
Just like that, it was over. They hit the corner and was outta sight. I looked next to me and saw my goons were still standing tall. None of us got hit.
"*No!*" I heard a woman scream from her heart. I already knew what that meant before I turned my head. A woman I had seen inside the house was holding a li'l boy in her arms while he bled out on the pavement. Rita ran over and started screaming, too, and that's when everybody came outta the house.
I walked over and saw the li'l boy was definitely dead. Multiple shots to the chest. This was the same li'l teenager that was just runnin' around, so full of life. I locked eyez with Ms. Wallace. *See why they gotta die?* I thought, like she could actually hear me.

She gave me a knowing nod.
The sirens came, then we were gone.

Marcellus Allen

Chapter 10

One week later

It had been so many shootings since that weak shit those cowards pulled in the Ville that I'd lost count. The town was lit and wasn't nobody safe, and I mean nobody at all. Those Gutta Squad faggots were hittin' back hard, especially Pressha. That nigga was on a warpath about his baby mama. Every time I turned around, he was either shootin' up one of my blocks or shootin' up a trap house. I wasn't worried about his heartbroken-ass, though. It was like we were playing chess, but on two different levels. He wanted pieces, I wanted the king.

I wasn't able to do nothin', though, but sit back and take it while I planned my revenge. That monitor was killin' me slowly in more ways than one. I knew the pigs were just waiting on me to slip up so they could throw the book at me. I think they were sitting at their computers, watching my movements all day, just hoping I fucked up. I almost did with that hot shit in the Ville, but my lawyer ate that shit up. Yeah, I was in the Ville, which is huge, that don't mean I was a part of no shooting, though. They were hot about that and I knew it, so I didn't do nothin' but record music, spend time with my fam, and spend money. I couldn't meet up with no clientele or nothin'!

I came from the streetz, so there wasn't no way I was letting them crackers stop my hustle. All I did was adjust my program.

The day was somewhat dark and gloomy, even though it was barely past four o'clock in the evening. The rain was beating down on the car windows with a vengeance as I drove me and Spike through the city. Today was the day we were meeting with Def Jam. I thought me being on the monitor and not being able to fly to L.A. would kill the sit-down, but it didn't. Spike had managed to convince them to hold the meeting in Portland, so we were headed downtown to the Hilton to conduct the business.

"Why you looking at me like that? I already told you I'ma take the vest off once we get there," I said after watching him look me up and down from the corner of my eye.

"You got all that jewelry on for a business meeting like we going to meet the connect or somethin'. We wanna present you as a man that knows how to conduct business, not a street thug," he spat.

This nigga serious? I thought to myself. "Blood, we ain't going to buy a restaurant or no shit like that. We going to see how much these crackers wanna give me to rap about being a gangsta. Shit, if anything, I'm living up to their expectations. On the real, though, you need to fall back on all that extra shit," I replied.

He shook his head and mumbled somethin' under his breath that I couldn't hear.

Spike was my nigga, but ever since he moved to Atlanta and started blowing up, he had turned real Hollywood on me. I had always heard about the shit happening, but figured it didn't happen to real niggaz. I had been wrong about that, but I made a vow to myself that day I would never sell out and go Hollywood. I was a street nigga to the core, and couldn't nothin' on this planet ever change that. Nothin'!

We pulled up to the Hilton twenty minutes later without saying another word to each other. I took my vest off like promised, then followed him to the Presidential Suite where the powers-that-would-be were waiting on us. Soon as we were let inside, I instantly knew I wasn't gon' like these crackers. I don't know what it was, but I could tell if somebody was flawed right from the jump. They looked like snakes in suits.

"How are you doing, Mr. Anderson? I'm Steven Welch, head of A&R for the urban market," he extended his hand.

A white boy leading the urban market?

"How are you doing? I'm William Brewer, V.P. of marketing," the other white guy extended his hand.

I shook both hands, sized them up, declined a drink, then sat on the couch. For the next thirty minutes they explained how they came across my music, how the label wanted me, and then the contract terms. For the most part I just listened while they did the talking. The only thing I was concerned about was the money.

"Also, Mr. Anderson," Steven said, then paused until I made eye contact with him, "I don't know what it is that you're doing, but you're going to have to stop," he demanded while taking in my attire.

I lifted my red bottoms in the air until the monitor came into view. "You talkin' about this?" I asked with a smirk on my face.

"That, too," he frowned, "but I'm speaking about all the jewelry and expensive clothing you have on."

I screwed my face up. "You want me to dress different?" I asked, faking ignorance.

"Not that, but whatever you're doing to be able to pay for it needs to stop. I'm guessing that's at least $200,000 worth of jewelry that you're wearing," he said.

At least, I thought.

I was done playing with them crackers at that point. It was a few things that weren't adding up to me financially-wise that needed to be addressed. I guess they thought I was the dumb rapper and Spike was the business man. I leaned close to the edge of the couch so I could stare right in their eyez. "Earlier you said my advance would be around 200 thou, right? For three albums? After all they are recuperating and what not?" I asked.

"That's right, and you get that the moment you start working on each new album," he said and smiled.

"You also have your royalties, too," the other one added.

"Right, of course. But after all the recuperating and shit, I doubt I'd have too much left. I mean, that does happen a lot, right?" I smiled.

"Only with low sales. We're expecting you to go platinum the first year, so that won't be a problem," Steven defended the label.

I put my hand under my chin like I was in deep thought. Like I was seriously thinking over the offer.

"You said I had over two hundred thousand in diamonds on me right now, right?" I asked.

He nodded slowly at me.

"Then why would I wanna sign my life and rights over for what I have on right now?" I grilled him.

They both were surprised. I could see it on their faces. This was the part of the meeting where I was supposed to be grateful and ask where was the pen so I could sign the dotted line. "I don't think you understand the opportunity we're giving you right now. This is a contract from Def Jam, and this is a good deal," Steven spoke with a red face.

"One million dollars," I spat.

"Excuse me?" he asked like he just knew his ears had to be deceiving him.

"I said I want one million up front for all my hard work and troubles." I looked him right in the pupils.

I saw Spike shaking his head right next to me. I didn't give a damn how he felt.

"We're not going to be able to do that," he said with an air of arrogance.

"I'm making a million with or without you. Have a nice day," I replied, then walked out without looking back or speaking another word.

I sat on the hood of my car for five minutes before Spike came rushing over like a linebacker. "That was dumb as fuck, nigga!" he growled at me like I was a li'l nigga.

"How high they go up?" I asked, totally ignoring his li'l outburst.

"Another hundred grand," he relented.

"You ready?" I jumped down and opened the door. I was over the shit and had more important things to do than be discussing three hundred thousand to sell my soul.

Spike was still standing in the same spot with a mug on his face.

Fuck wrong with him? I wondered. I was done catering to his Hollywood ass. I slammed the door, then got right up in his face. "Blood, it seems like you got some shit on yo' chest you wanna get off," I spat, ready to deal with it man-to-man right then and there.

He did the unthinkable and pushed the shit outta me. I was so caught off guard, I stumbled back a couple feet. When I regained my balance, my hand went straight to my hip outta habit. *I left the gun in the car,* I thought. He was lucky I did, 'cause I probably woulda left his ass dead in that parking lot. "You must be tired of living, nigga," I spat with venom.

"Naw, nigga, I'm just tired of you! I'm tired of you fuckin' everything up with that fake-ass John Gotti attitude you've got. You're starting to let that li'l money and power go to your head," he shot back.

It took everything in me not to reach in that car and come out bustin'. I had to remind myself this was my nigga. A man

I used to look up to, but I felt devils tingling inside of me. "What you getting outta this deal?" I smirked, finally understanding why he was mad. "You talkin' all that money shit, but you the one going Hollywood with yo' bitch-ass. I know you made some type of side deal with yo' greedy-ass. If this was the streetz, you'd be a dead man walking for what you did," I chastised him.

He got back in my face. "Well, kill me, then, since you such a fuckin' goon," he growled, tryna show some heart.

"Blood, you know dis ain't what you want. Don't forget I ain't no rap nigga. I really bury niggaz." I let my nutz hang, too.

He stared me down like he was actually debating poppin' off. He ain't never been no bitch, but he ain't ever been stupid or suicidal, either. "I'm done fuckin' with you, Blood," he said, then turned around, walking away.

"Naw, I'm done with you, you fuckin' sell-out!" I yelled after him. *Fuck that nigga,* I thought as I hopped in the 'Rati.

***

"Well, put ya 3D glassed on then, pussy, 'cause you know we comin' straight at you!" Beanie Sigel yelled on the screen, pumping me up.

After I decided to spare Spike's life on behalf of the dead homies, I went home and chilled with the fam. Me and Olay were on good terms, and I was tryna keep it that way.

"I want some ice cream, Daddy!" Mar-Mar yelled out.

"You know yo' mama ain't about to let you eat no ice cream while she's cooking dinner," I said.

"You tell her, then," he demanded. He crossed his arms and stared me down like he was some type of boss.

I laughed in his face. "Don't let this movie get you up, li'l boy. There's only one king in this family, and that's me. Got that?" I play-punched him.

"I thought I was king, too, Daddy?" He smiled like he knew he had me.

His li'l badass too smart. "You are a king, but not until you're a grown-up. So right now you're the prince," I explained.

He looked at me like he was tryna read me or somethin'. The way he cocked his head to the side made me believe in DNA. That was exactly what I did when I was analyzing somebody. The way my son acted and how much he looked like me amazed me every single time.

"The prince wants ice cream!" he demanded, then punched me back.

"The prince gon' get his ass beat," I said, then went back to watching my favorite movie.

Ten minutes later Olay came halfway down the stairs with her phone to her ear.

"Burnside at the front gate, baby," she told me.

"A'ight, send 'im down here, and take this heathen with you," I responded.

"Okay, daddy. And dinner almost ready."

"Baby, why this li'l boy been tryna con me into bringing him some ice cream down here?"

Soon as I said it, my son looked at me like he wanted to fight, then started shaking his head at Olay. "Uh-uh, Mama!" he pleaded.

"Tell her how you the prince, and you demand some ice cream," I added.

"Boy, get yo' badass up here and wash up for dinner, and hell naw you ain't getting no ice cream," she punked him.

He jumped off the couch with an attitude, then turned around before reaching the steps. He flinched at me, then said, "Ooh! You snitch, Daddy!" He was dead serious, too.

"Get up here! Talking about somebody snitchin'," she said, then got back on the phone. "Yeah, girl, he was talking to his daddy," she said, then started laughing as she headed up the stairs.

I got up and turned the lights on so I could see his face while he got 'some shit off his chest,' like he claimed he needed to do. He had surprised me when he called, talkin' 'bout we needed to have a face-to-face. I guess he was starting to pick up on the vibes. Either that or his guilty conscience was starting to play tricks on him. I patted my waist, making sure that thang was there. *Just in case.*

"What's Mobbin'?" he said, walking down the stairs.

"Steady Mobbin', the usual," I replied, shaking him up. I tried to get a read on him. He definitely looked like a lot was on his mind. *What else you hiding?* I didn't sense no aggression coming from him, though. I went and sat down on the couch while he sat across from me. The only thing that was in between us was my big-ass chessboard. The irony of it was not lost to me. Maybe him, neither.

I put the TV on mute and got straight to the point. "So, what's on yo' mind, Blood?" I asked.

"I don't know how to explain it, but shit ain't been the same since you came home. It's like you ain't fuckin' with me like you used to. You got me and Joe on the outside, lookin' in," he said.

I wonder why! "I don't like the way y'all was runnin' shit when I was gone. It looked like you were tryna take over shit from Gotti. Putting all yo' key niggaz in key places. Not to mention yo' relatives from Jersey. They should've never overseen nothin', especially the money," I gave it to him raw.

"I can see how it could look that way," he said, then nodded slowly, taking it all in. "But don't I get the benefit of the doubt? We've been rockin' since grade school, and I ain't never tried to play you. Ever!"

Except for now! That's why you over here tryna rock me to sleep. I know you killed Boobie, nigga!

"I've put my life on the line every day for this Mob shit ever since we started it. I've been right there with you from day one, building this shit up from the ground. So, if I overstepped some grounds, then my bad. I was just tryna keep this shit alive while you were gone," he pleaded his case.

Play a sucker to catch a sucker, I reminded myself.

I wrestled with myself internally about my next move. I was tired of playing the sneaky games with this nigga and was ready to get it over with. Obviously he was starting to catch on, and that made the stakes even more deadly. *I'ma kill this nigga right now,* I thought as I eased my gun from my waist under the table.

"I understand, brody, and my bad for not just sittin' down with you man-to-man." I paused while he nodded his head, really thinking I'm a sucka. "I do got an important question for you, though, 'cause some shit just came up that my lawyer just told me."

"What's good?" he asked.

"That night me, you, and Joe hit that spot on Flavel, what happened to the smacks? I'm asking cause the shit just came up and I need to know our bases are covered. We usually go dump 'em, but for whatever reason we forgot to do it that night. Some snitch told the cops it was our team, so we gotta cover our tracks," I put out there for him. I gripped my banger even harder and slid my finger on the trigger. It would have to be now, and I was more than ready.

He was deep in thought, tryna figure somethin' out. "You know which gun it was?" he asked, looking genuinely confused.

"I can't remember who had what gun. All I remember is somebody had a .9 with a laser on it," I said, playing dumb. *Just shoot this nigga and get it over with,* my inner goon told me.

He snapped his fingers. "That's right! The .9 with the beam on it. It was all chrome, too. That muthafucka was chunky. Yeah, that's the one I had that night. I remember now," he said.

My heartbeat sped up as he admitted to having the gun that killed my best friend right in my face. I lifted the gun a li'l higher.

"Where is it?" I asked and held my breath. *Take a deep breath. I know what I'm doing.*

"I gave it to Joe the next day. He was talkin' about he wanted to use the beam before we got rid of it. I told 'im to make sure he dumped it that week," he said with sincerity.

I prided myself on being able to read people, especially my own homies. Everything I was reading was telling me he was telling the truth, but Burnside was a street veteran, and a nigga can't master the streetz without learning how to lie.

"A'ight, call that nigga and find out what he did with it and the one he had. It's important we hurry up and cover all our tracks before it's too late," I lied.

"A'ight, I'm on it," he pulled out his phone and called Joe on speaker.

He didn't show the slightest hint of anxiety or guilt. I still kept my eyez glued to his hands, though, just in case, 'cause shit can change in the blink of an eye in this dirty game. Burnside was the most ruthless nigga I knew, so I wasn't taking no chances with my life.

"What's poppin' slime?" Joe answered.

"Yo real quick, did you get rid of that chrome .9 with the

beam that I gave you? The one from that one night?" he asked.

My heart was jumping out of my chest while I waited on the reply. *If he don't say the right words, then I'ma crush this nigga right now.* I mentally prepared myself to shoot one of my closest friends in the head. *This is for Boobie,* I had to pump myself up.

"I been dumped both of those thangs in the river, son. Why you asking 'bout that?" Joe answered.

"I'll tell you in person, Blood. It's nothin' though, just making sure all our bases are covered cause snitchin' at an all time high right now. I'll clap back," he hung up.

I let my gun fall to the floor just like my heart did at the same time. My world came crashing down. I almost killed my nigga for somethin' he didn't do, and he didn't even know it. Some Meek Mill lyrics popped into my head:

Oh, what a feelin' when you and ya homie chillin'
And you know he probably got thoughts of robbing and killin' you.

I felt like the biggest snake in the world at that moment. I was preparing to take my brother to war when he did nothin' wrong. I killed my own men preparing for this war! *I'll never forgive myself for killing Flip and Major,* I thought. I instantly felt like throwing up when I remembered how we did them. *They told me they didn't know nothin',* I reminded myself. I'd never felt lower than I did at that point.

"Yo, O, you a'ight, nigga? You look like you just saw a ghost," Burnside brought me back to reality.

"Yeah, I just need a drink. I've been stressed out," I said, then went to the bar and poured myself a drink. *I was lookin' at everything all wrong,* I thought as the Cîroc burned my chest. One thing I wasn't looking at wrong, though, was the fact Jersey Joe had to die. He had been the puppet master the whole time. He was the one tryna take over my shit.

I kept tryna figure out why would he kill Boobie first, if that was the case. Then it hit me like a ton of bricks outta nowhere. It was the oldest reason on earth, and it never failed to amaze me. The graveyard and prisons were packed to the maximum behind them.

My best friend was dead behind a no-good bitch.

The anger I felt at that moment wasn't comparable to nothin' I'd ever felt. It was blood in my eyez.

Chapter 11

"What the fuck you mean, Burnside ain't the one who killed my brother, dawg?" Twin yelled, jumping up from the couch. "I knew some fuck-shit like this was gon' happen, shawdy. That fuck-boy killed my brother, and now you wanna protect him!" He pounded his fist in his palm as he spoke.

I had to take a deep breath and count backward from ten before I shot his dumb ass in the head for disrespecting me yet again. I had called an early morning meeting at my house so I could tell them what I found out the day before. I stayed up all night tossing and turning, sick to my stomach and tryna plan out my next move. Here I was, ready to get the shit off my chest, and this li'l nigga was tryin' me.

Don't kill him. He's just emotional. You would be, too, I thought to myself. I had to go pour myself a shot of Cîroc, and I never drank in the morning. I watched Gotti pull Twin back down on the couch. Bleed just stared at me, waiting for me to finish.

"Like I was saying." I walked back over and stared Twin in the eyez. "Burnside ain't the one that smoked Boobie. It was that sneaky nigga Joe." I gritted my teeth. Just saying the words made venom run through my veins.

I saw the confusion on their faces and the wheels turning behind their eyez. "How you find out?" Gotti asked the million-dollar question.

For the next ten minutes I broke down in vivid detail how everything transpired leading up to Burnside calling Joe. When I was finished, all three of them were shaking their heads. We were all thinking the same thing.

"So we killed our own team for nothin'?" Gotti brought the question into the light that was killing me in the dark.

I dropped my head. "Yeah, we did," I mumbled.

"Fuck, Blood!" Bleed yelled, then started pacing the room.

I knew exactly how he felt. That night I didn't get no sleep and I shed a tear, but I did promise myself I was gon' make Joe pay for it in the worst way possible. I had plans on torturing his ass.

"We still did the right thing, when you look at it with your emotions detached," Twin spoke up.

We all turned our heads at the same time, muggin' him. *Nigga, what?*

"Hear me out, shawdy." He put his hands up in surrender so we'd listen to 'im. "Y'all said they were more loyal to Burnside than the rest of the team, right? So, either way, we were gon' have to pop they top, no matter how you look at it, dawg. Think about it!" he said.

"How the fuck you figure that? 'Cause I'm not following you, nigga," Gotti spat in his signature deep voice.

He didn't understand, but I did. I knew exactly where he was headed with the shit. I instantly got a headache from just thinking about it. Some slick shit I heard Jay-Z say before popped into my head about how this game would make a young nigga feel old.

"He's saying we're still gonna have to kill Burnside," I said in an annoyed tone.

"Exactly," Twin confirmed my nightmare.

"Why would we have to smoke him?" Bleed wanted to know.

I sighed. "'Cause he ain't gon' be coo' with us crushin' his favorite relative, that's why," I broke it down.

"I don't give a fuck how he feels about it! His family shouldn't't've killed our nigga over no bitch! He better get with the program," Gotti spazzed out.

"He won't, and you know it."

"He might if we show him the proof. Ain't no getting around that," he tried to reason with us.

I shook my head. "He won't believe it. He'll just come up with some excuse how Joe didn't do it. Them niggaz are like brothers," I pointed out, feeling my headache getting worse.

"There's gotta be a way to handle it without us killin' the homie. He's our brother," Gotti pleaded.

He was right, and the whole situation was destroying me inside. I couldn't think straight while my emotions were runnin' wild. We were discussing killing one of our own men for somethin' he didn't even do.

"We can kill Joe and make it look like the Crabs did it," I finally said.

"That'll work," Gotti responded way too quickly.

"I'm killin' da bitch, too, dawg. She ain't exempt. She probably pumped up the fuck-nigga to do it," Twin growled.

Fuck, I didn't even think of that. Now Olay gon' be sick, I thought while shaking my head. I told Falon if this shit happened, then I was gon' pop her top, too! She didn't take heed, so her ass was about to get smoked, too. "Yeah, she definitely dyin' with his bitch-ass," I signed the death warrant of a woman I viewed as my li'l sister.

All I kept thinking about was how her death was gon' break Olay down to the ground. As much as I wanted to spare her the heartache, I knew I couldn't. There were rules to this shit that nobody was exempt from. *I warned her,* I thought of Falon.

"This shit is fucked up, Blood. The whole situation," Bleed voiced what everybody was thinking.

"I'm ready to avenge my brother. I can deal with the aftermath later. Boobie in a casket over a funky-ass bitch, dawg. I ain't got no remorse, shawdy," Twin stated his point of view.

Later that day I was pushin' the Maserati through the town, collecting money and tryna clear my thoughts. That's all I could do since I had that fuckin' monitor on. Pick up money and record music, that's it. I never knew how much I enjoyed being in the mix until I was forced outta it. I actually wanted to do some large-scale drug deals. I wanted to feel the rush of exchanging the work for the money. I wanted to feel like I was getting one-up on the feds. But most of all, I wanted to purge on my enemies. They were gon' feel my presence as soon as that bracelet came off.

They thought they was doing somethin' while I was outta commission. *We'll see,* I thought as I honked the horn. I pulled up to the spot Phatz was in charge of. Li'l Bobby's funeral had passed a few days ago, and I wanted to check up on him. Plus he was really showing me where his heart was at by the way he was out there bustin' his pistol. He had bodied one of those li'l nobodies from Gutta Squad, but that was a start. The li'l killer was starting to really grow on me, and I felt like it was time to take him under my wing, 'cause the rate he was going at was gon' most definitely get him a life sentence.

Phatz came out with a duffle bag, jogged down the steps, and hopped in the whip.

"Here go the loaf, and it's all there," he said while handing the bag over.

"I already know it is." I tossed the bag on the back seat. "Yo, I want you to roll around with me today. Go tell them other niggaz to hold it down," I told him.

"A'ight, hold up." He jumped out and went back in the spot.

It was time I started getting hands-on with my young niggaz. Most of the ones we had pumping for us I didn't even know who they were. I had become detached from the ground level, and that was dangerous in this game. That's why everybody loved Boobie. He stayed in the streetz. He loved spending his time with the li'l niggaz, grooming them. He drove old-schools and rocked hood gear. Me, I was the exact opposite in everything.

"Where we going, big homie?" Phatz asked, getting back in the car.

"Collect the loaf from a few spots and just ride around. You good with that?"

"I'm with whatever you is," he replied.

We'll see, I thought, then pulled off.

For the next twenty minutes we listened to Kevin Gates while driving through the town. I took everything in and processed it one thing at a time. Block-by-block, face-by-face, I took it all in. I could always tell who the wolves were and who the sheep were. They could try to hide behind the tough-lookin' faces and hoodies, but real recognized real. That killer shit is either in a nigga's eyez or it's not. *Those niggaz be fakin' it.*

"Don't waste yo' energy. They're nobody," I told Phatz when I saw him grip his gun in his lap.

We drove by some li'l niggaz that were playin' thug on the block. They called themselves, throwin' up their hoods after we drove by.

"You see what hood they threw up?" he gritted in anger.

"I saw that Gutta Squad shit. They wanted to look hard in front of their li'l bitches. Let 'em."

"Fuck that! They killed Bobby and Boobie, so it's on sight until they all dead," he spat.

I pulled the car over and parked. "That's where your thinkin' is messed up, li'l bro. Fuck the li'l niggaz. Killin' them won't mean nothin' to Butta and Pressha, trust me. All you gon' do is get a life sentence if you keep torchin' all their pawns. I'ma show you how to kill the head, and then watch the body fall apart. I know that anger you're feelin'. Trust me, I do. Now, I can show you how to become a made man, or I can circle around this block and you can go shoot up some nobodies. Which one you wanna do?" I asked.

"I wanna do it the right way," he answered.

I smiled, then leaned my seat back like I didn't have a care in the world. He looked around nervously, then focused on me.

"You know why I can park on this or any other block without a care in the world?" I asked.

"'Cause niggaz is scared of you. They know what will happen," he stated with conviction.

"You mean they fear me?" I clarified.

"Yeah, they fear you." He was certain.

I shook my head. "Wrong. It don't got nothin' to do with fear. Don't get me wrong, niggaz fear me, and that's good to a certain extent, but wolves don't fear nothin'. So, when I ask you that question, I've got the wolves in mind," I said.

"Then I don't know the answer," he gave in.

I spread my arms and smiled at him. "'Cause this car is bulletproof," I said.

"Huh?" he was confused.

"I know the real killers don't fear me, and they're not supposed to. I've been shot too many times and done lost too many homies to ever feel that way, so I bossed up and made myself bulletproof. That's what made men do. We could sit here all night listening to Pusha T while them dummies shoot at us, and we'll never get hit. That's why I can drive slow through any hood without giving two fucks. I'm tryna elevate your level of thinking," I said, then started the car back up and drove off. "Oh, and the Crabs didn't kill Boobie. Jersey

Joe did."

"What?" he yelled out.

"Sit back and listen while I break it all down to you," I said, then started from scratch. By the time we pulled up to Mallory Courts fifteen minutes later, I was done explaining to him everything that had happened. The only part I left out was us killin' Flip and Major. That still didn't sit right with me, and the last thing I was about to do was open up sore wounds.

He sat there shaking his head and grinding his teeth until I was finished. "I never liked that nigga ever since that one day he kept tryna get you to kill us. When y'all murk his bitch-ass, let me pop him one time for Bobby," he said.

I nodded my head at him. "What you think about Burnside, though?" I wanted to see where his head was at.

"I think it's playing a dangerous game, either way. If he finds out we killed Joe without bringing it to him first, then he gon' suit up on us. If you bring it to him first, then he ain't gon' believe it, especially since nobody actually saw him," he answered, mirroring my exact thoughts.

"So, what's the best move?"

"Killin' Joe and making Burnside think the other side got 'im," he said.

I nodded my head in agreement. I knew that was the best solution, but I still felt wrong for keeping it from him.

"C'mon, let's go," I told him, then jumped out in the cold. I put my hands in my hoodie as we crossed the street, heading to the apartment complex.

It was crowds of people standing around each corner like always. The Mallory was weird like that. The drugs didn't get sold inside the complex like most places did. Instead they got sold outside the gates and all around the four-block radius. No hood actually claimed it as their own. It was closest to the Unthank Park territory, but far enough where they didn't wanna have the headache of regulating it, even though they slid through there multiple times a day. It was technically a free market, but it was always some new li'l click tryna edge their way in. I dropped off bricks to my man Block and let him deal with the rest.

I pushed the intercom to be buzzed in and looked around while we waited. I noticed Phatz had his hand around the handle of his heater on his hip. *He ready.* I smiled at the young braveheart.

The gate unlocked and we made out way through the complex to Block's door. It was opened up before I could knock by a sexy chocolate chick I assumed was his newest piece. "He's in the back room, waiting on you," she said with a smile, leading the way.

I couldn't help but take a few peeks at her ass while it jiggled in those booty shorts. *I'd fuck her,* I told myself.

Block was sitting on the floor, counting money with a money counter when we walked in. He had a few piles all around him. He was definitely getting to the bag. I fucked with him the long way.

"Big O-Dawg, what the business is?" he greeted me in his usual overly-happy tone.

"Shit, steady Mobbin', like always. I'ma pick that up right now and have one of my goonies bring the pack by later on," I replied, then accepted the blunt he handed over to me.

"Tisha, bring me a paper bag in here!" he yelled out to her. "I already got yo' 45 bands counted out over there." He pointed to a pile in the corner of the room.

I coughed a few times, then passed the blunt to Phatz. "Oh, by the way, this my li'l nigga, Phatz. I'm grooming him to take over one day," I nodded toward Block.

They nodded and shook hands. Block's girl came back in

and started putting the money in the bag.

"What's new out here? Any problems from the young niggaz outside?" I asked.

"Naw, everything is Gucci around here. I sell 'em zones, and they pill-for-pill it and come back for more. It's easy money for me," he replied.

His girl handed me the bag, then left the room.

"A'ight, I'll tap in later with you," I said, then we blew the joint. On our way out of the door, I just had to turn around once we hit the hallway to check if she was lookin'. She was, just like I figured. *Big bank take li'l bank.* I smiled as I closed the door, but kept eye contact. *I'll catch up with her later.*

When we got outside, it seemed like all eyez were on us, but I was used to that. I looked to my left and saw a group of teenagers shootin' dice with their li'l girls standing by them. *I remember those days,* I thought as we crossed the street. I watched a young hustler serve a fiend on the corner we were approaching.

"It's still a gold mine out here," I said out loud to myself.

"We should take it, then!" Phatz spoke for the first time since we got out of the car.

Soon as I opened the door, I heard a voice yell out, "Yo, big homie!"

I tossed the bag on the seat with my left hand, then pulled the heater with my right and spun around. Phatz pulled his out and stood in the street, ready for whatever.

"What's Mobbin', nigga!" I had the .40 aimed right at his face.

He put his hands in the air. "No disrespect, fam! We just wanted to holla at you!" he pleaded his case. His homies were looking surprised as hell and caught off guard. The li'l bitches wanted to cry.

I tucked my heat once I realized they meant no harm. "Y'all know who I am?" I asked.

"Yeah, you OG. O-Dawg from the Mob," the li'l hustler said. The rest of the crew nodded their heads in agreement.

I crossed the street and walked up on them. "What's yo' name, li'l man?" I asked.

"Li'l Mann. I'm from the Clack Unit," he said proudly.

I was surprised I accidently called him by his name, but I was even more confused by the Clack Unit name. I didn't know what the hell that was. "Clack Unit, huh? What is y'all? Bloods? Crips? Hustlers?"

"We Blood." He threw up the 'B' with his hands, then his homies follow suit.

I nodded at their gangsta. "What y'all wanna rap about with me?"

"We wanna take a picture on yo' car," he said with a straight face.

"On my car? Everybody gon' know it ain't yours," I asked, not even tryna hide my confusion.

"We want a group picture by yo' car for Instagram and Snapchat. You driving around in our dream car, and that shit inspires us. We wanna be like you one day and take it to another level. That's all we want, big homie." He made his case, and his homies were nodding their heads like he was preaching or somethin'.

This is why Boobie stayed in the streetz so much. I was expecting them to ask me for a hand-out or to let them join the winning team. Hell, I was expecting anything but a picture. That fucked my head all the way up. I didn't even know how to respond to that. His words really played on my heart. Those few words touched my soul. To know I was somebody's inspiration was crazy to me. I was used to the hate, the gunshots, gold diggers, and the groupies, but never the next generation looking up to me. I looked at Phatz to make sure he was hearing the same thing as me. He tucked his gun and shrugged his shoulders.

"A'ight, y'all come on. And don't be scratchin' my paint, either," I gave in.

They all broke to my car with smiles on their faces, fighting for the best spot. They spent over five minutes taking pictures and switching positions. It was pure comedy to me. I actually cracked a smile.

"Thanks, O-Dawg," Li'l Mann said, then shook my hand. His whole crew shook me up next.

"You good, li'l dude," I said, then looked at the li'l girls. "Can y'all wait across the street while I talk to the men?" I told them. Once they were out of hearing distance, I addressed the group. "I respect y'all hustle and get-down to the fullest, believe that. Stick together and stay loyal and y'all will make it in this game. Yo, Li'l Mann, how old is you?" I asked.

"I'm seventeen," he answered.

I thought he added an extra year, but let it slide for the time. "When you hit eighteen, then come holla at me and I'ma get you right. I don't let minors put in work for me, my nigga. That my own moral rule. This the devil's game, so I don't like corrupting children, but –"

He cut me off. "I'm already corrupted, big homie," he said.

"I believe you, my nigga, but my rule is between me and God. Once you turn eighteen and you wanna play the devil's game fo 'real, then I'ma show you. But I am gon' do y'all one solid that I usually don't do. I'ma hit y'all with a half a brick for free, no strings attached at all. I'ma have it dropped off tonight, so be ready. After that, I can't fuck with y'all no more on that level until it's that time, so don't even ask.

A'ight?" I said.

"I understand," Li'l Mann said, then the rest agreed with him.

I saw the looks in their eyez that were so familiar to me. There were gon' get money and be in the streetz until they died. That choice had probably been made years ago, but I still didn't like puttin' kids on. I stared at the five young hustlers and saw me and my squad a decade earlier. It was do-or-die with us then, so I knew they were on the same trip, too. Time and jail time would tell.

"What's up? Can the Mob shoot dice with y'all, or what?" I asked, breaking the silence.

"I'ma feel bad takin' yo' money, big homie, but don't trip. I'ma hand it over the fireplace," Li'l Mann said, then started laughing. They all did.

The next few days flew by with no street drama or home drama, and that was a first. Maybe the holiday season had everybody on chill mode, but I knew it wouldn't last long. I felt like the enemy was lyin' back in the cut, just waiting to strike. With Pressha's baby mama being killed, I knew not to ever let my guard down. That nigga was out searching for revenge.

"We going outside, Mama!" I yelled to my mother, who was in the kitchen cooking. She had called me and my brother and demanded we bring over her grandbabies, so I brought my son, Jaxx brought his two daughters, and we chilled out while the kids played with each other.

"I'm glad you're still alive, li'l nigga," Jaxx said while he pulled a blunt from his pocket. We sat down at the table in the backyard.

"Why wouldn't I be? I'm a beast out here in these streetz," I shot back, full of arrogance.

"Y'all definitely been out here tryna purge any and everybody. It's that damn Mozzy music," he laughed and hit the blunt.

This nigga. I inhaled, then exhaled real slow, calming myself. "You ain't seen nothin' yet. Wait until I get off restrictions. We murkin' everything moving on some 100 days, 100 nights-type of shit. Just wait," I said.

"100 days, 100 nights? Fuck is that?" he screwed his face up.

I sucked my teeth at his ignorance. "The shit that was poppin' off in L.A. in 2015 when niggaz went a hunnid days straight of ridin'," I explained to him.

"You niggaz going to the feds!" he busted out laughing.

"Maybe, maybe not. But if we succeed, then most of yo' competition gon' die out, too. They big spenders gon' be lyin' in a coffin, which is gon' hurt they pockets. That means everybody that buys from Gutta Squat, Murda Squad, Sixties, and whoever else want beef gon' have to cop from me now. Which means the more weight I gotta get from you," I broke down.

His eyez got wide and I saw the dollar signs appear in them. *Now he feels me.*

He finally passed the blunt, then rubbed his palms together like he was Birdman. "See, now you talking my language: money. That's what we're supposed to be in this shit for. Everything else is for the birds and ain't never made since to me. Now you onto something, and if you need me, you know I got the line on the guns. I'm talking that big shit," he offered.

Now he on board all of a sudden. "I thought we were going to the feds?" I coughed and gave the weed back.

"Oh, that was different," he said, mimicking DJ Pooh from *Friday.*

We busted out laughing at the same time. The weed made it ten times funnier, and I couldn't stop myself if I wanted to. I was bent over at the waist, laughing and coughing at the same time.

My phone went off. When I saw Burnside's name flash on the screen, I just knew somethin' was wrong for some reason. I could feel it in the air. "What's Mobbin'?" I answered.

"They just shot up Joe's Escalade in the Jack-in-the-Box drive-through. He got grazed in the face, and the bitch Joy he was with is in critical condition," he spoke without breathing.

"Fuck! Where's Joe at?" I asked.

"Hiding in some bushes. I sent Shanell to go pick him up."

"Meet at the Mob quarters tonight. Bring yo' two relatives, too. It's that time, Blood," I said, gripping the phone even tighter.

"Say less. Mob out," he said.

"Mob out," I responded and hung up.

I shook my head at the irony of the situation. I was mad somebody tried to kill the nigga who killed my best friend. It was a dirty game we were playing. I wasn't trippin' 'cause I played for keeps, as they were about to find out.

I looked at my brother. He shook his head and walked off.

Chapter 12

We ended up meeting at the warehouse that night instead of the Mob Quarters 'cause Rugar was there and I didn't want him bein' a part of this meeting. I was done fuckin' around with those pussies, and they were about to find out. We were in the same basement where we killed the white bitch at. I was standing in the exact spot.

"Yo, son, I'm tellin' you, them niggaz is mad pussy, word is bond. I was stuck between two cars, and they didn't run up and get the job done. They ho-asses was shootin' from thirty feet away like they Steph Curry or somethin'," Jersey Joe stood in the middle of the room telling us.

Everybody laughed like getting shot was funny. Twin was the only one with a mug on his face. I made eye contact with him and shook my head real slow, letting him know to be calm. He nodded, then looked away.

"You sure it was those Rollin' Sixty niggaz?" I asked for clarification.

"I'm sure, son. I looked them cowards right in the face. It was Big Lurch and Face. Word is bond. I'm not trippin', though, 'cause the bitches gon' think this shit is sexy, word is bond." He started rubbing the big-ass bandage that covered half his face. He didn't wanna chance the hospital, so he had one of his bitches patch him up. He looked like Frankenstein's monster.

"They weak asses finally decided to do somethin'. Fuckin' Crabs," Bleed spat.

"Well, they fucked up big time, 'cause ol' girl is Li'l Capone's baby sister," Gotti said while staring at his phone.

"What?" Burnside yelled out in surprise.

I was surprised, too. I thought she was just some square chick that didn't know nothin' or nobody. I thought back to when we first met her and her homegirl at that Footlocker the night of my concert. *Sneaky bitch,* I thought.

"What you say, son?" Joe needed to hear it again.

"Those suckaz been on here shootin' shots about the situation. Li'l Cap just made a post about that being his sister. It's going down on here right now," Gotti let us know.

"Fuck that bitch, son. That's what she gets. Yo, I think she was tryna line me up," Joe spat.

That had definitely crossed my mind when it first came up. I threw it out, though, after adding it all up in my mind. Either way, it didn't matter no more at that point. We had more important things to discuss. "I doubt that's the case, but either way, they struck first, so y'all know what time it is. We gon' have to get the Capone nigga out the was ASAP," I spoke up.

"Who is this Capone nigga, son?" Beast asked.

"An enemy that got some heart in him, nothin' special. Fuck 'im," Burnside spat his usual arrogance.

"100 days and 100 nights," I said, confusing everybody.

"Say what?" Burnside asked.

"Soon as this monitor comes off, we're going hard for exactly 100 days and 100 nights. No days off, none of that," I said.

"We on Cali time now?" he smiled at me.

"That's exactly what we on. We knockin' everything down that's moving, period. If they don't buy dope from us or rock with the Mob, then they food. We settlin' all debts. So get to doing y'all homework on them niggaz so when it's time to purge, we can do it right," I said.

"I can't wait for this shit, Blood!" Burnside got all excited.

Everybody started talkin' their shit, how they gon' pop this nigga, what gun they gon' use, what blocks we shootin' up. All the talkin' had me ready to go right that night. The shit gave me chillz. I loved it. It was about to be wartime, and there was nothin' I did better that put pussies in the graveyard. I loved counting money and loved to spend it even more, but it was somethin' about being a war tactician I just loved more than anything. I smirked to myself 'cause I was plottin' another war only a few knew about.

Fuck it, it ain't my fault. I'm just dealing the hand I was dealt. I nodded at Joe when he stared at me.

***

Three weeks later

I pulled up to the parole and probation office feeling like a new man. I usually avoided going downtown, especially early in the morning, but this morning was somethin' to celebrate. They had to take that damn monitor off, and it wasn't shit they could do about it. They asked the judge to prolong it, but my lawyer ate it up. It was a wrap. I walked into the cracker's office and put my feet in the air like I was King Tut or somebody from a royal bloodline.

Just when I thought it was a perfect morning, the house niggaz walked in with three bitch-ass gang cops. "What's up? Y'all want my autograph?" I asked with a smile on my face.

"We came to warn you," Detective Rogers said.

"I appreciate it, I really do." I felt like being sarcastic. I hated black cops.

"We know all about your li'l 100 day and 100 night campaign. It's not gonna fly, so you can take that shit back to California."

Damn, niggaz stay snitchin' out here, I thought, but played it coo' on the outside. "I don't know what the hell y'all talkin' about. Y'all pigs just made that shit up so y'all can harass me 'cause I'm black with money. 'Cause I actually do hard work and not eat doughnuts all day," I shot back.

"He's playing the race card, fellows," Sgt. White joked with his fellow swine.

Somethin' about the gang task just really irked my nerves. I hated them muthafuckaz more than the Nazis. I looked him dead in the eyez so he could tell I meant what I had to say. "I sure hope you and the rest of these pig bitches didn't plan on using none of y'all vacation and sick days, 'cause I'm about to make you punks earn what li'l pay the state gives you," I spat, getting their full attention. "So keep laughing over there like I'm some type of bitch or somethin'. You muthafuckaz ain't seen nothin' yet, I promise you," I threatened.

Nobody said nothin' for a full minute, just stared each other down. They knew at that moment they were dealing with a real psychopath. I could see the fear in their eyez.

"Why don't you tell that coward friend of yours, 'Jersey Joe,' to be a man and turn himself in. It's only so long he can hide," detective Freeman said, making quotation marks with his hands when he said his name.

"He not hiding, he just prefers to hold court in the streetz," I replied. Joe had been all over the news the last week for that shooting at Jack-in-the-Box. Joy had come outta a coma and snitched on him being the shooter who jumped out of the truck, getting away. *Rat bitch.*

"We'll see about that," he replied to save face.

"Yeah, we will. You're about to see a lot of things," I said, then got up, flexing my leg real slow to tease them. "Make sure y'all dress warm," I added, then walked out on they bitch-ass.

I sent a text message to one of my new li'l bitches, letting her know I was on the way. First I went and met up with Twin and Phatz at the studio to make sure they had their heads on straight. It was about to get real, and I needed to know they were ready. I needed Twin to keep his emotions in check, 'cause it was almost that time.

"Yo, dawg, I'm good," Twin told me in frustration when I explained it to him. I was sitting at my desk while they both sat across from me, looking annoyed.

"I'm serious, Blood. I need you to be able to hide yo' emotions better while we're out in the field. Wolves pick up on shit like that. It's almost over, so just bear with me," I explained to him again.

"I said I'm good, shawdy," he responded.

"Phatz, this about to be a lot of pressure on you that you ain't used to once we squeeze that first shot. Just know we ain't stoppin'," I told him.

"I'm ready to earn my keep," he vowed.

I knew he was the one.

"I'll holla later. I got new pussy on the line." Wasn't nothin' else to be said. It was go-time.

I pulled up to her spot in some apartments off 162nd and Glison Street and honked the horn. I gripped the .40 in my lap just in case some fuckery was in the works. *I don't trust no bitch,* I reminded myself. I looked around to make sure it wasn't no niggaz tryna creep my ride. I had used the same tactic too many times to ever fall for that shit. *Yeah, right!* New pussy was a muthafucka and had been the 'cause of many great men lyin' in the ground.

I was all man and couldn't help myself when she slid in my DM. I knew I was gon' hit it in due time.

I unlocked the door and let her in. Her perfume instantly filled the car up and got my dick hard. I gave her a quick glance before I peeled out. She was looking super sexy with a trench coat on and some red fuck-me pumps. I wanted to know what she was wearing underneath it.

"Hi, daddy. I love this car," she smiled and purred at me.

"You a bad bitch, Tisha. What you got on under that?" I complimented her.

"Thank you, and you'll see," she flirted.

"I knew since I saw you at Block's house that I was gon' have you." I felt like being cocky.

"I wanted to fuck you right then and there," she shot back with no shame.

After she hit my inbox with her number, I immediately got on her. We texted for a few weeks, and then it was a wrap. She was ready to do whatever I wanted her to do, but I just wanted some new pussy. I planned on hittin' it a few times, then giving her back to Block. I didn't need no new bitches on my team. The two I had was a handful by themselves, so I was good. Plus they were solid bitches.

But the dawg in me wanted to sample this thick-ass chocolate bitch. I couldn't help it. I didn't feel no type of way about fuckin' Block's bitch, either. He bought dope from me, that's it. He wasn't Mob and didn't have no family ties, so fuck 'im. He better respect the rules: a bitch always gon' choose the nigga with the bigger bag, period. It came with the game, just like death and prison.

"Oh yeah? What about now?" I pulled my pants down and whipped my dick out. I was done talkin'. "Can you handle this?" I challenged.

She licked her lips and leaned over. "You better put yo' seatbelt on," she said, then licked the head with her tongue ring. She licked my balls one at a time, then licked back up to the head and swallowed the whole thing.

"Oh, shit!" I yelled out. She surprised me when she took

the whole dick without working it down. I put my hand on the back of her head and enjoyed the show.

Slurp! Slurp! Slurp!

She slurped and bobbed her head like a porn star. She went all the way up, then back all the way down. I could feel her throat gripping me and my head touching the back of it.

By the time we made it to the Marriot, I had busted in her mouth, and she swallowed everything like the freak she is. I took her into the room and found out she only had on a g-string set under that coat. I fucked her in the jacuzzi, the bed, couch, and floor before I took her back home on cloud nine. She was talkin' about how loyal she would be to me and would do anything for me. *Yeah, right.*

***

Christmas came too soon, and it was a hell of a day. I had to take Olay and Mar-Mar to my mother's house to be with the rest of my family, then slide over to Tamia's parents' house and deal with her crazy-ass family. Olay kept threatening that if I brought Tamia over, then she was leaving for good.

"She gon' have to be able to come over eventually. She's having my daughter. You gotta be reasonable," I had told Olay.

"No, the fuck she ain't coming over. I don't ever wanna see that bitch, and she can't come around the family or my son. To us, her and that baby don't exist," she spat.

"My kids are going to be around each other, Olay," I told her.

"Yeah, when they're eighteen," she shot back.

I was mad as fuck, but decided it was pointless to argue with the crazy bitch. My kids were going to be around each other on a weekly basis, no matter what she was talkin' about. If she didn't like it, then she could kick rocks, 'cause wasn't no way in hell I was letting a bitch run my program, especially concerning my kids.

Now Tamia, on the other hand, wasn't trippin' at all over the petty shit. "Long as you don't treat us like we're not family and your mother accept your daughter, then I'm coo'," is what she had to say.

I told her she had nothin' to worry about 'cause that would never happen. On top of that, my mother was extremely happy about my daughter, so everything was Gucci. Above everything else, the children were happy and that's all that mattered at the end of the day. I spoiled both of my bitches with diamonds for their presents, then it was back to the trenches.

The day after Christmas I jumped back in the studio and finished the last song on the mixtape called *100 Days, 100 Nights*. I shot at all my enemies and maybe even made some new ones. *Fuck it.*

Rugar released my *Blood In My Eyez* mixtape that day, and the streetz went crazy. I got over a thousand downloads the same day and was the talk of social media. Even niggaz I didn't fuck with was showing the mixtape love, but of course the opposition was on there, hatin' like always. They claimed I was dry-snitchin' and started calling me all types of snitch again. I found that real funny since those same niggaz be praising Half Dead as a real nigga. *We about to find out if they really about what they claim they about,* I promised myself.

Chapter 13

New Year's Eve

One up top, ahky. Somethin' stocky in the choppy,
Fat wally for bradaski, off a oxy, bet he mop 'em.
Pour a four of wocky, vision cloudy, sleep walkin'.
Pour a four of wocky, vision cloudy, sleep walkin'.
Aye, we done came a long way, traveled down the wrong way.
They ain't find no shell cases, thankful for the cold case.
The Mozzy song got turned down, snappin' me outta my zone.

"What's taking her ass so long!" Phatz said after turning the volume down. He was sitting behind the wheel, so I guess he felt like he was in charge of the music. Bleed looked at him like he was crazy from the passenger's seat. In Portland, it was against the law to turn off Mozzy in the middle of a verse.

I just looked out the window into the nighttime darkness, tryna spot Falon, but I couldn't see her nowhere. We were sittin' in the Astro Van five-deep inside the Kit Kat Club parking lot. Me, Bleed, Gotti, Twin, and Phatz. Burnside, Joe, Premo, and Beast were parked right next to us.

"I told you about having patience, li'l nigga. There's a time and place for everything, and right now is our time. Trust me, Falon will get it done. I ain't never seen a nigga turn her body down," I lectured him.

Not even two minutes later, Gotti blurted out, "There they go, right there."

I looked out the window and watched her and a big, buff nigga walk in our direction. He was so caught up with watching her huge ass wobble he didn't even notice how deep in the parking lot she had brought him. No witnesses, no help, and low lighting. I felt my anger rising the closer he got.

Take a deep breath. I know what I'm doing.

I slid the door open and bounced out like I was part of a SWAT team or somethin'. By the time he looked up I was right there, five feet away with the .45 aimed right at his chest. I didn't have no mask on 'cause I wanted him to recognize me. I seen in his coward eyez that he did.

"Remember I told you what would happen if you tasered me?" I growled at him.

He put his hands up in surrender. "I was just doing my job," he pleaded.

"And now I'm just doing mines."

Boom! Boom! Boom!

I literally saw the flame jump out of the barrel. He grabbed his stomach while he fell to the ground.

"Argh!" he screamed out like a bitch.

"You ain't so tough without ya boyz, huh? You big bitch! I brought my boyz with me, too." I stared at his weak ass, then turned toward the van. "Yo, Phatz, come here." I waved him over.

He hopped out and walked over with no hesitation at all. "What's good?" he asked.

"Kill this pussy for me," I demanded. Everything about the li'l nigga told me he was a killer, but I needed to see it myself. Up close and personal, the ultimate test for a killer. A lot of niggaz shot from across the street and got lucky. Some catz just shoot to wound a nigga, not really wanted to catch a body. To be a part of my circle, a nigga had to be a killer, period.

He pulled his head and aimed at his face.

"I got kids!" muscle man yelled.

Boom! The bullet knocked half his face off and made his head bounce off the concrete.

I knew it! "Fuck yo' kids," I said. *Boom! Boom!* Then I put two more in him 'cause he was a bitch.

I looked at Falon stuck in place, then broke back to the car and we blew that joint. After we got a few blocks away, my adrenaline started to slow down, and I was able to lie back and relax. *I told 'im what would happen.* I wanted to hurry up and get his ass outta the way. He wasn't a threat at all, but my pride wouldn't let me let it go, so I used him to clean the dust outta my gun and test Phatz. Both things were in order. *Now it's time to play fo' real,* I thought to myself.

"Y'all popped the shit outta his bitch-ass, on me. I should've got out and popped 'im, too!" Bleed said outta nowhere.

We all started laughing, breaking the tension. The car had been dead quiet since we drove off. Our hearts had been beating too fast to say anything.

"You 'bout to have a whole lot of niggaz to shoot in a minute, soon as we get there," Gotti spoke up.

"100 days and nights is officially on the countdown," I announced. "Twin, you Gucci?" I asked.

"I'm good, dawg," he replied, then started playing with the choppa on his lap.

I already knew what was on his mind, and I fully understood. I couldn't wait to avenge my brody, either, but I knew it was a time and a place for everything. *It's almost time.*

"I like how you handled that, Phatz. No hesitation at all. That's that Mob shit right there, Blood," I complimented my young goon.

"It was nothin'," he replied, real nonchalant.

I can dig it, I smirked to myself.

The night was young, and we were just getting started. The enemy had their turn, but now it was ours. I couldn't do shit for thirty days, so now it was their turn to be preyed upon. The whole town was about to feel where I was coming from. *They should have killed me while I was on the sidelines. Now I'm on they ass,* I vowed.

"Y'all remember, no man gets left behind. We going in as a unit, so we're coming out as one," I spoke to the group as Phatz parked the whip.

The second van parked right next to us and we all hopped out and huddled up behind the vans. "I can hear 'em from way over here," I told Burnside. We were standing across the street from the Rockwood Apartments in a bar parking lot. The Rockwoods were a known hangout spot for the Crips. We had gotten word the Sixties were throwing a New Year party inside of them, so we invited ourselves.

"Yeah, they think this shit is a game," Burnside said, then cocked his Mack 10. "Let's bring the New Year in the right way."

I nodded, loving his gangsta shit. "Y'all take the left side, and we got the right. I don't know what apartment they in or how many they got, so just follow the sounds and shoot to kill," I instructed.

Multiple guns being cocked back was the only reply I got. I pulled the Freddy Krueger mask down over my face, then cocked back my .45. I had replaced the standard magazine with a fifty-round drum. I was ready for war.

We crossed the street with guns hanging by our legs like we were in some fuckin' third-world country or somethin'. We didn't give a fuck about nothin' except for killin' somebody. I looked over to my right at Twin holdin' the AK across his body like he was with the Taliban. I tried to get a read on him, but couldn't. It was always hard to read what he was thinking.

As soon as we reached the complex, some nigga jumped outta his car with a bottle in his hand. "Where the homies at, cuz?" he asked, assuming we were with the Crip party.

What a dummy, I thought. The shit was so stupid I couldn't even shoot him. I just laughed behind my mask.

"I don't know, but they'll be joining you real soon," Burnside said, then popped him.

Boc! Boc! Boc!

The nigga fell back on the trunk of his car, then dropped the bottle in slow motion. It shattered while he held his stomach, tryna stop the blood from pouring out. He was so confused he didn't know what to do. Beast and Premo walked up, finishing him.

Bloc! Bloc! Bloc! Bloc!

Boom! Boom! Boom!

He did the Harlem Shake, then slid down the car, dead to the world. Joe shot him in the face, making his body roll over. *Boom! Overkill!*

"One for us, zero for y'all. That bouncer didn't count," Burnside said. It was a challenge.

I looked at him, smiling behind my mask. We'd done this before when we first came up in the streetz. We nodded at each other, then took off runnin'. He took all the apartments on the left, and I got the right. I heard my team right behind me and saw the others across the lot right behind Burnside. We were on some Call of Duty shit, but wasn't no restarting the game for the dead men. We were playing for souls.

I slowed down when I saw a group of people sittin' on stairs and leaning against cars. They were so caught up in the music blasting from the car and passing blunts that by the time one of them looked up, it was too late. He didn't even warn his homies. He jumped off the ledge, knocking one dude down, and hauled ass. I stepped to the side so Twin could step up.

Yoppa! Yoppa! Yoppa! Yoppa! Yoppa! Yoppa! Yoppa!

Them AK rounds destroyed everything they came in contact with. They hit one cat in the back so hard he did a flip frontward and came down smokin'. *Damn!*

Boom! Boom! Boom!

Boc! Boc! Boc!

We joined the party and started tearing their asses up, too. One of them busted back at us as he ran inside an apartment. Soon as we rushed behind him, somebody started dumpin' on us from down the lot. From the sounds of it, I knew it was multiple niggaz bustin' on us.

"'Sup, cuz!" one of them yelled out.

Boom! Boom! Boom! Boom!

Burnside and them bum-rushed 'em while they were focused on my team. *I'll holla,* I thought, then ran into the open apartment lookin' for something to kill. We looked everywhere, but it was a ghost town. *Where the hell he go?* I asked myself after I opened the bathroom door.

"He ran out the back door!" I heard Gotti yell out. We made our way to the living room where the patio door was halfway open. He had escaped us.

"Bitch-ass nigga!" Bleed yelled out.

I could still hear the gunshots coming from outside, so I spun around to go help my squad. Soon as I took the first step, that's when the shots started.

Boom! Boom! Boom!

The glass shattered on the patio door, and I hit the floor to dodge the bullets that were coming at me.

Bloca! Bloca!

Boc! Boc! Boc!

My niggaz got to bustin' back while I jumped up and got

out of the way.

"He runnin', Blood! I'm 'bout to get 'im!" Bleed said then ran outside, shootin'.

I nodded at Phatz, and he ran after Bleed. The rest of us ran back to the parking lot to assist the homies. I damn near tripped over a dead body laid out in the hallway. *Yeah, he dead,* I thought as I stared into his lifeless eyez.

Boom! Boom!

We hit the parking lot as Joe stood over somebody, delivering the fatal shot. He put his arms in the air like he just scored the winning touchdown. "Got 'im, coach! That's the last one!" Joe yelled out.

Boca! Boca!

We all got low when we heard the shots. *Must be Bleed,* I told myself. Then him and Phatz came runnin' from around the complex, all outta breath.

The police sirens could finally be heard in the distance. With all the fireworks and random gunshots going off, the pigs didn't know what to do. We didn't stick around to find out. We broke.

We pulled up to the 6 West Club in Vancouver 45 minutes later. We changed clothes and cars, then came through to party just like everybody else. While them pussies were scraping their homies' brains off the ground, we were ballin' out, bringing in the new year.

"We been here all night, right?" I asked the security guard who let us in the side door.

"I personally let y'all in as soon as the doors opened up," he said, his eyez never leaving the thick knot I had in my hand.

"My man." I handed over the money with a smirk.

We walked in like we owned the spot and showed them niggaz in there what it was to really ball out. Everybody bought at least two bottles then we took over VIP, like we always did. All the bad bitches flocked to us like they were supposed to do. They knew when real niggaz with money was in the building.

I got so caught up in the partying and poppin' bottles that I totally forgot we had just crushed an apartment complex. That's how it went in the concrete jungle. A nigga kills in order to live to see another day. Then he eat again.

Chapter 14

One Week Later

The streetz were on fire, and it wasn't nothin' nobody could do about it. Bodies were getting dropped left and right on a daily basis. Gang task didn't know what to do! It seemed like every gang in Portland was in on the 100 days, 100 nights movement. Niggaz was tryna purge, fo' real. Whatever beef a gang already had, it got ten times worse. The Hoovers and Rollin' 60's were on at each other. The Inglewood Families vs. the Six Deuce Crips and the Sixties. The Mob vs. Gutta Squad Piru. The niggaz that were left tried to slide a few times, and it was too many li'l new chicks that were beefin' to even count.

I couldn't tell who was winning and who was allied with who. The shit was real triv to the highest degree! Me and my goonz were out lurkin' every day, so it was only right we took a few hits. First the Sixties popped Premo in the chest while he was sitting at a red light. He lived. It was nothin'!

Then some fuck-niggaz went and shot up Li'l Bobby's mama's house. I didn't see the point in that since he was already dead. We figured they wanted to send a sign of disrespect. We got it loud and clear! Wasn't nobody more disrespectful than us!

"Make sure that thang already cocked back. You know niggaz be up here," I told Phatz as I parked at the Rose City Cemetery.

"This muthafucka stay cocked in the house. It's too triv out here right now not to be ready," he replied in all seriousness.

We hopped out four cars deep at the side of the cemetery. This was where niggas parked if their loved ones were buried at the back of the cemetery. There was a side entrance they could use instead of going through the front and having to take that long-ass walk.

I had the .45 with the drum poking outta my hoodie just in case shit got real. It was an unusually hot day for early January, but that's how Portland weather was: hot one minute and pouring down rain the next.

"Here the grave go, right here!" Burnside yelled from about ten rows down.

I walked over with the quickness and looked down to make sure. *Yeah, this his bitch-ass!* I thought while I pulled my iPhone out. *Y'all wanna be disrespectful, huh?*

"Yeah, we live from a bitch-niggaz' current resting place. He was a rat alive, now he's a bitch in death," I spoke into the camera, making sure my face was visible.

"Don't trip, you snitch-ass nigga. We gon' send yo' homies real soon," Gotti spoke up.

"Half Dead ain't half dead no more. He fully dead now! Hot nigga!" Bleed jumped in.

Everybody took turns talkin' shit on camera, but that wild-ass nigga Beast took the cake. He turned it up a notch.

"Aye, y'all step back, son," he said, then started unzipping his zipper. We all got back fast! *This nigga trippin', Blood.* He pulled out and got to drowning Half Dead's headstone! I recorded every second of it while all of us laughed our asses off.

"This how we get down in Jersey, word is bond!" he laughed while he shook the last of his piss out.

Boom! Boom!

I got down low when I heard the shots, dropping my phone as I reached in my hoodie.

"Joe! What the fuck, nigga?" Gotti yelled at him.

"I found the pussy-nigga Ron's tombstone!" he yelled

back, gun still smokin' in his hand.

Boom! Boom! Boom!

Boc! Boc! Boc!

Now Twin joined the action, followed by the rest of the gang. They shot the shit outta those two headstones. I wasn't about to record them doing that, so I aimed the phone at my face instead.

"Y'all still wanna be disrespectful? Bitch, the Mob Life runs Portland! I'ma see y'all real soon. Mob up or get shot down!" I yelled over the shots.

Boom! Boom! Boom!

The sirens started coming, and that's when we started going. I was laughing all the way back to the car. *Fuck them pussies!*

"Let's hit up the dispensary and get some weed," Phatz said after we had been driving around for thirty minutes.

I had posted the video all over the internet, and them niggaz were hot! I probably got about fifty death threats in that time period. I found it funny and made a post telling them exactly that. We were already at war until the last man was dead, so I didn't understand why I was supposed to be scared over a threat. *We'll see.*

"I don't know why everybody wanna get they weed from the dispensary now. Just 'cause them crackers done made it legal don't mean we gotta buy it from them," I said, then busted a left down Sandy Boulevard. I was one of those catz that still preferred to get mine from the weed man. I didn't trust those Europeans with my weed.

"Fuck what you talkin' about. They got the most fire, period. I'm tryna get high, then catch one of those Crabs slippin' for shootin' my aunty house up," he replied.

We pulled up to the Treehouse Collective on 24th and Sandy twenty minutes later. I had to park on the street since they didn't have no parking lot. I didn't think twice about my Maserati standing out in that part of town. That's where all the rich whites lived at, and the reason I chose to hit that weed shop.

"This damn drum won't fit all the way in this hoodie," I said, getting frustrated. I sat there tryna adjust the gun so none of it was sticking out. It wasn't happening. The drum was too fat. *I should've brought the stick with me.* "Yo, I'ma post out here 'til you get back, 'cause I ain't going in there like this. Just bring me back some of that cookie everybody be talkin' about," I said, giving up and placing the heat back on my lap.

"Uh-uh, can't do it, big homie. They only let you buy an ounce at a time, and I'm getting a whole zip of that fruity shit. Just leave the heat in the car. It's only gon' take us two minutes," he said.

I debated it for a few seconds 'cause I really didn't like leaving my pistol nowhere, especially in the middle of funk season. I needed some weed to calm my nerves, though. "A'ight, c'mon, li'l nigga." I gave in and put the heat on the floor.

We got in there and he couldn't decide on what type of weed he wanted. It must have been a hundred different types of weed to choose from. I started to get a headache from tryna read the names on every label. *Fuck this!* I told the cashier to just let me get an ounce of that cookie and I'm good. Phatz took forever tryna do the most, but finally decided on a mix of three different weeds ten minutes later. We threw our weed in their li'l weed bags and got up outta there.

I noticed a Jeep parked across the street as soon as I walked outside. For some reason it didn't blend in with the surroundings to me. It looked like a G-ride, and that could only mean one thing. I jammed my hand in my hoodie looking for the smack. *Fuck, it's in the car,* I cursed myself. I sped my pace up. "Watch that Jeep, Blood," I told Phatz.

"I'm on it," he spoke real low as the Jeep started up and drove down the street.

My heart was beating fast as a muthafucka. I just knew that was enemies in that car. *I be trippin' without my thang,* I told myself.

"You need to hurry up and get high, 'cause you on some paranoid shit. I almost just went to jail for dumpin' on some innocent white people," he said.

"I know," I responded, then started laughing with him.

Screech!

I looked to my left and saw the same Jeep hittin' its brakes in the middle of the street. My heart started pounding as the doors flew open and Butta, Pressha, and Pull Out bounced out with guns on them. My heart was telling me to try and hurry up and run to the driver's side so I could get to my gun. My mind was telling me it wasn't no way in the world I was gon' make it without being shot, and I should run.

We were standing by the passenger side, about five feet away. They were in the middle of the street, ten feet away from the car.

"Bust, nigga!" I yelled and got low.

Boom! Boom! Boom! Boom!

Boca! Boca! Boca!

Bloc! Bloc! Bloc!

Boc! Boc! Boc!

All the guns went off at one time, sounding like a bomb had just went off. Phatz was standing up behind the car, letting that thang go the fuck off! He showed no fear.

"We here, cuz!" Pressha yelled out.

I popped my head up and saw them gaining on us with one purpose in mind. I saw it in their eyez. They knew they had us.

Boom! Boom! Boom!

Phatz ducked down next to me, and that's when I grabbed him. "We gotta run for it, Blood! We got one gun!" I told him.

He was ready to die, I knew that look all too well, but I was tryna live to see another day. *When you ain't got a gun, then you run,* Jaxx's words to me when I was a li'l nigga popped in my mind.

"We'll get 'em another time!" I said, then took off runnin'.

He busted a few shots to keep them back, then followed right behind me.

Boom! Boom!

Boca! Boca! Boca!

Bloc! Bloc! Bloc!

I swear I could hear the bullets flying by my head and felt the heat off them. *Please, Lord, let me make it,* I silently prayed.

"Argh!" Phatz yelled out, then bumped into me. I knew he was hit. When I turned around, he was on one knee. We were right at the corner, almost there. We locked eyez. *I can't leave him.*

I ran over and helped him up, and that's when they smelled blood in the water.

Boom! Boom! Boom!

Phatz spun around and started bustin' back while I was still holding him. Then he got hit somewhere in the chest, and it caused both of us to stumble back. He slipped outta my arms and fell on his ass.

"Get outta here, nigga! I ain't gon' make it, and I plan on

dyin' like a real nigga!'" he yelled at me.

That shit touched my soul and boosted me up! He started shootin' from the sitting position. I saw them getting closer and closer. *Fuck that! Ain't no bitch in me!* "No man left behind," I yelled back, then scooped his ass up.

Boom! Boom! Boom!

Boc! Boc! Boc! Bloc!

I dragged his ass around that corner while he was shootin' with one hand. Once we hit the corner, we ran as fast as possible down the street until we crashed into a coffee shop. I laid Phatz on the ground and took his heat.

"Somebody call the ambulance. He's been shot!" I screamed out.

The shop was damn near empty, which was a good thing. An older white dude with an apron on came over and started helping me keep him elevated. "Emily's calling them right now. Just stay alive, bud!" he said, then started taking Phatz' shirt off.

I heard the sirens and remembered I had his gun on me. *Shit!* "I gotta get rid of this thang. I'll see you at the hospital," I told him.

"Fuck them niggaz. I ain't dyin'." He said it like he meant it. I knew he was gon' fight for his life. I knew he wasn't gon' die. I just felt it.

I ran up outta there and got to my car as fast as possible. The pigs were pulling up right as I was leaving. Shit was triv.

***

The next day I got a phone call from Gotti early in the morning talkin' about the Gutta Squad having a barbecue in Irvington Park.

"Nigga, what? I'm leaving the house right now. Tell

everybody to suit up!" I couldn't believe my ears. My li'l hitta was lyin' in a hospital bed with an IV hooked up to him and they wanted to eat chicken? They had been all on Facebook talkin' that goon shit about how they did us? I just knew somebody had given Gotti some bad information. It couldn't be.

By one o'clock that afternoon we were locked and loaded and parked across from the park. Me, Bleed, Gotti, and Twin were in one car, and Burnside, Joe, Beast, and Premo were in the other. Premo was back in the action even while his chest was still recovering. Some people just live for the gunplay. It's a natural high.

"I still can't believe these niggaz is out here like this," I growled. I looked out the window and saw a couple of faces I recognized as the enemy. We were posted up by the entrance across from New Seasons. We could see by the small basketball court and where the BBQ grillz were at. We hadn't seen any of the main three that we wanted.

"They feelin' themselves right now. It's coo', though. We fixin' to shut this shit down, on me!" Bleed shot back.

"Yo, hit a couple blocks so we can see if these pussies are even here yet. Go by the other basketball courts, Blood," I told Gotti.

He pulled off, and so did the other car. I stared at everybody in that park with hatred. They was out enjoying the sun while it was out, having a good time like shit was coo'. My pride and ego were begging for revenge. I had embarrassed myself the day before, chased down the street like a li'l bitch! They should've known I was gon' come back shootin'.

"There they go, right there! Butta fat ass playin' ball," Gotti said.

That was music to my ears right there. I looked out the

tinted windows and saw exactly what I didn't expect to see. *They really out here.* I shook my head. I saw Pull Out runnin' down the court on the opposite team. Pressha was standing in the grass a few feet away, surrounded by some niggaz that was about to find out how real shit was.

"We hoppin' out, crushin' everything. If those niggaz ain't in it, then they is now. They knew it's triv time. We in and out 'cause the boyz be hot around here. Don't go too deep in the park 'cause they got us outnumbered, especially with all those other catz on the other side of the park," I instructed, then slid the door open.

I bounced out with the Draco and a fifty-round banana clip and my Teflon vest on. I had on some black sweats and a mask, that's it. No shirt, hoodie, or none of that shit. I was on some ready-to-die-about-it type of shit.

We all crossed the street with our guns out and hearts set on murder. I pulled my mask up. "Y'all still lookin' for us?" I yelled, then slid my mask back down.

It seemed like the whole park froze up at the same time. Their fear had them stuck in place.

Doom! Doom! Doom! Doom!
Boom! Boom!
Boca! Boca! Boca!
Boc! Boc! Boc!
Bloc! Bloc!
Doom! Doom!

We had it sounding like the Fourth of July. All them pussies on the court hit the deck immediately. A few cats who were just standing and watching the game moments ago were now laid out, bleeding from their mouths and heads. We weren't doing no bullshittin' with 'em. We were crushin' shit! Bodies were twisting and turning everywhere. Finally, Pressha and two niggaz he was standing with started bustin'

back. *I can always count on ya!*
Boom! Boom! Boom!
Boc! Boc!
Doom! Doom! Doom!
All of us focused our fire on them three, eatin' they ass up! One of them got hit in the chest, and his gun flew outta his hand before he dropped to the ground. Pressha and the other cat put some distance between each other, but kept shootin' at us. I kept my baby choppa aimed at Pressha. I wanted that body bad.
Boom! Boom! Boom! Boom!
Boc! Boc!
Butta, Pull Out, and some other cat joined the firefight. We spread out a li'l bit and kept walking slowly toward them. Any and everything that popped in our line of fire got put down. Pull Out wanted to be the braveheart out of the bunch by walking toward us, shootin'. His clip went empty and he tried to pull another from his shorts, but we weren't going for that! We applied the pressure and sent 'im runnin'

He had almost made it to the bench when a bullet struck his back. He flew a few feet forward and fell on his knee. He popped up and tried to dash behind the bench, but fell short due to multiple gunshots that tore into him. He hit the ground right under the bench and stayed there.

The sirens hit the soundwave, and they seemed closer that they should be. We turned around and sprinted up outta there. Them cowards kept shootin' at our backs, but we weren't trippin' 'cause we accomplished our goal. I actually got to see the look of devastation in Butta's eyez as he watched his li'l brother drop for the last time. Now that was priceless.

As soon as we made it out of the park, two police cars were pulling up to the scene. *Fuck,* I thought. My mind tried to hurry up and come up with a decision. *Try to make it to the car, or run?*

Boom! Boom! Boom!

Boc! Boc! Boc! Boc!

Burnside started serving the boyz, then Beast joined in.

Doom! Doom! Doom! Doom!

Boc! Boc! Boc!

I left off the Draco, then everybody got to bustin' at 'em. They put their cars in reverse and tried to get up off the block. The windshield glass got knocked out in the process.

"C'mon, Blood!" I yelled, then ran to the whip. I knew we had about thirty seconds before the whole Portland Police Department showed up. We hopped in and smashed out.

I lay on the floor, heart feeling like it was pounding out of my chest.

Marcellus Allen

Chapter 15

A Few Days Later

We laid low for a few days after we escaped that shit. We were on fire! Everybody and they mama was on Facebook dry-snitchin'. We were masked up, so I knew couldn't nobody point me out, but I was still on eggshells. I went and got a room out in Seattle until I knew it was Gucci in the town. I had Tamia calling the jail twice a day to see if I had a warrant. None of the pigs got hit, so that made some of the heat die down a li'l bit.

Pull Out's bitch-ass was on his way into the ground to hang out with the rest of his dead homies. Every time I thought about him, it brought a smile to my face. I just hoped my bullet was the one that purged him. They were so sick on Facebook, it was pure comedy. Now he was the realist nigga to ever come outta Portland! Niggaz kill me.

I drove back to the town early in the morning after confirming again that I had no warrants out for me. Nobody knew I was back except Twin, Bleed, and Gotti. We had business to attend to that couldn't wait.

I picked up Twin and Bleed and then headed to Falon's house. I called her earlier and told her I was sliding by so we could have a heart-to-heart. We pulled up around eight o'clock at night to her spot on Missouri, right off Portland Boulevard. She lived in a cul-de-sac coming off of a one-way street, which was perfect for what we had in mind.

"Let's go get to the bottom of this shit," I said, then got out into the cold weather. I looked into the night sky and stared at the full moon for a second. I got the chillz, but I wasn't sure if it was from the wind or from what had to be done. *I hope she don't know nothin',* I thought as I knocked on the door.

"What's good, brody?" she opened the door in some boy shorts and small tee.

"How you doing, sis?" I hugged her, then walked in.

"I didn't know you was bringing the whole gang with you," she said, hugged them, then led us to the den.

We all sat down and went quiet, not knowing how to start a conversation that was going to change our lives.

She looked at each of us and immediately got alarmed. "Please, don't tell me Joe is dead!" she panicked.

"Not yet, shawdy, but he will be," Twin spat. I could tell he was offended by what she said. Those were the last words he wanted to hear.

"What the fuck you say? Get out of my house!" she yelled while jumping off the couch.

He pulled out his .357 and aimed it right at her heart. Fear instantly set in, and she looked right at me. She was pleading with her eyez.

"Sit down, li'l sis. We got a lot to talk about," I said, then eased her back down into her seat. *Here we go.*

"What we gotta talk about where y'all bringing guns into my house?" she asked with an attitude.

I turned my body so I was facing her head-on. I looked deep into her eyez and gave it to her raw.

"I know who killed Boobie, and so do you. The secret is out now, and I've got the proof. He made a crucial mistake. What we want from you is to tell us why he did it," I said.

"What are you talking about? The Crabs killed Boobie, and everybody knows it," she lied. I seen it all in her eyez, and her body language told on her.

Dumb bitch, I shook my head.

"She lyin', Blood," Bleed said how he felt.

Before I could reply, Twin jumped off the couch and

jammed the heat in her mouth, forcing her head back. "Tell me more lies on my brother, bitch! Yo' fuck-ass nigga killed him over you, didn't he? Didn't he?" he yelled at her.

She was tryna say somethin', but couldn't get it out due to the gun in her mouth. I pulled his arm away and told him to fall back. She went into a coughing fit for a few seconds.

"Li'l sis, you only making this shit harder than what it needs to be. You're my son's aunty, so I'm not gon' kill you, but you need to tell me the truth. Twin deserves to know why his brother is dead. If it was Olay, then you would feel the same way. C'mon, sis," I switched tactics and started playing on her emotions. I felt bad for a split second, doing my li'l sis like that, but she did it to herself. *I told her ass.* I hated being in that position, but these were the cards I was dealt.

"I'm sorry, brother. I really am." She looked at me with puppy dog eyez.

Here it is. My heart sped up with anticipation. "Just tell me what happened," I said.

"I didn't know he did it at first. He used to always say he was gon' kill him, but I never took it serious. He used to say he was gon' end up killin' him 'cause he was in the way of our love. Then they kept beefin' over small stuff, but when Boobie punched him in the mouth at the park, it was over after that. He was obsessed with killin' him after that incident. He didn't tell me he did it until after you went to jail and was there for, like, a month. He kept sayin' now we could be together, and he was gon' take over," she confessed her soul.

Me and Bleed locked eyez, then shook our heads at the same time. It was one thing to know the truth and another to hear the truth. *This shit crazy,* I thought. "Take over how?" I asked, already knowing the answer.

"He said while you were in jail, Burnside was gon' be in

charge. Which meant he was gon' be more in charge, and they were going to keep flying in their family from Jersey to run things," she said and sniffed back tears.

I shook my head at the truth while I texted Gotti. *It's time*, I wrote him, then got back to Falon. "A'ight, here's the deal, li'l sis. You 'bout to hand yo' phone over so we can text Joe to come over here ASAP. We killin' his ass, bottom line. You getting outta town tonight, and I don't wanna see you for at least a year. Understand?" I told her.

"Yeah, I understand. I'm so sorry I didn't listen to you, brother." She started cryin' again.

"Where yo' phone at?"

"On the table in the front room," she answered.

Bleed went and got it, then came right back and sat down. "Code?" he asked.

"Sixty-nine ninety-six," she answered.

Bleed looked at her and smiled. *Freak bitch,* I thought.

He typed for a few seconds, then put it down. "It's done," he said.

Less than a minute later her phone started going off, but we were expecting that. I had hoped the text would be enough, but I stayed ready. That's why I had pumped her up the way I did.

"Answer it. Just remember it's either him or you," I warned her.

Twin aimed his gun at her while she answered it. She looked scared to death, but that's how I wanted it.

"Hello? It is an emergency. No, get yo' ass here right now, because I'm scared! Some niggaz pulled a gun on me in the Safeway parking lot, and they tried to follow me home, but I shook them. I'm here with all the lights turned out, waiting on you to get here! Come now, Joseph! Okay, bye," she hung up.

She played that role way too good, I thought. Somethin' told me she had used her skills on us. The looks my niggaz gave me told me they felt the same exact way.

"He's on the way right now. And he's with Gotti, too," she informed us.

"Turn off the lights, now," I told her.

She got up to do it, and Twin followed her every step of the way, breathing down her neck and just lookin' for any reason to blow her head off. Bleed went and stood by the window in the front room so we would know when they got there. The whole time we waited, Falon kept on apologizing to me and begging me to forgive her. Then she kept on telling Twin how much she loved Boobie and had planned on being with him forever. He stared right through her, not giving a fuck what she had to say at all.

Ten minutes later Bleed called out, "They pullin' up right now."

The anxiety was killin' me. I stayed up many nights in that cold cell waiting to avenge my nigga. My anxiety transformed into hate as I heard the door being unlocked. *Take a deep breath. I know what I'm doing.*

"Falon, whose Honda is that outside? Where is you at?" Joe called out.

The lights came on. He made it to the den and got the scare of his life: three known killers pointing gunz at him in his own house.

"What the fuck?" he yelled before hitting the floor. Gotti had crunched the gauge against the back of his head, knockin' him unconscious. Twin and Bleed took his heat, then cuffed his hands behind his back.

"Sit 'im on the couch," I demanded.

I looked at Falon, who had her hand covering her mouth, silently cryin'. I shook my head at her betrayal. *Bitches, the fall of men.* I prayed Olay and Tamia would never betray me like that, but I knew how humans operated. We'd do anything for the chance at surviving, for staying alive another moment.

"Didn't I tell you I was gon' ride for Boobie? Didn't I deliver?" I boasted to Twin.

He rubbed his palms in anticipation. "You did that, dawg," he responded.

I nodded, taking in the praise. "Wake him up," I said.

Twin smiled, then reached back as far as he could and slapped the shit outta Joe. It was so loud, I wouldn't be surprised if the neighbors heard it. Joe fell over to his side.

"Muthafucka! I'ma kill you!" he roared out.

Twin lifted him back up so he could look us in the face. We were sitting directly across from him.

"Go sit next to your nigga so you can tell him what you told us," I told Falon, who was sitting in the recliner next to us.

She looked scared to death. "Marshawn, please!" she whined.

"Bitch, get yo' ho-snake-ass over there before I cut yo' head!" Bleed checked her.

She looked at me for help, but saw no compassion in my eyez. She slowly made her way next to her man.

"Y'all always did look cute together," I cracked.

"Fuck you, faggot. Burnside gon' have yo' head for this, word is bond," Joe spat at me.

"I find it real funny you haven't asked why we're here, what we want," I said.

"What I want is for y'all to suck my dick, son. Ain't no ho in me." He looked me in the eyez to let me know he meant it.

He knows why we're here, I concluded. His arrogance

was making my blood boil like a muthafucka. It was like he was taunting us. Taunting Boobie. "You killed Boobie over this funky-ass bitch right here. Nigga, you a snake, and you gon' pay with yo' life, pussy," I told him his fate.

"Fuck Boobie! Before he died, he was a bitch. Now, like I said, son, suck my dick!" he yelled.

Twin smacked him in the face with the burner, spilling blood. "I'ma kill you, fuck-boy!" he yelled and hit him a few more times.

Bleed and Gotti started getting their licks in, too, turning Joe into a punching bag. I just stood there wondering how could I inflict the most pain on his bitch-ass. Then I got an idea.

I went to the kitchen and grabbed two of the biggest knives in the drawer. I returned to the scene with an evil smirk on my face. I looked at Joe's bloody face, and he still had the defiance in his eyez. I could respect that.

"You wanted me to suck yo' dick, right?" I held the knives up so he could see them. "A'ight, I got you," I said and saw the fear in his eyez for the first time. I handed the knives to Twin and started taking his pants off.

"What the fuck you doing, faggot?" he yelled.

"I'ma teach you about telling real niggaz to suck yo' dick, bitch." Then I yanked his briefs down.

"Yo, son, if you gon' kill me, then do it, but this ain't no real-nigga shit! Respect the code!" he pleaded.

I took a knife from Twin and started cutting his dick off. I was done talkin'.

Soon as the cold metal touched his meat, he started screaming for dear life. I kept on cutting. I was determined to bring the bitch outta him before he departed this earth.

His screams got even louder. Too loud. Gotti hit him with the stock end of the gauge, forcing him to hunch forward, wheezing for air. Bleed tilted his head back, putting him in the headlock and covering his mouth. Joe kept buckin' and going crazy, tryna get free, but it was pointless. I finally got the whole thing off, then stood up with it in my hand. Joe looked ready to faint.

"This what you turned yo' back on family for?" I asked Falon, then tossed the dick on her lap. She screamed while knocking it on the floor, then balled up on the couch, cryin'. *Stupid bitch.*

"We were good to you, my nigga, treated you like family," I told Joe while looking in his eyez. I plunged the knife deep in his side, then pulled it out just to do it again. I stepped back, lookin' at him in disgust.

"Fuck y'all." He barely was able to speak.

"Naw, fuck with us. Y'all get y'all licks in," I told them.

Twin went straight to work, stabbing him repeatedly. He was on some real Michael Myers shit. Bleed pulled out the knife I left and started stabbing him, too. Joe kept cryin' out the whole time. That shit was music to my ears.

When they got tired and stood back, I slit his throat, then stuffed his dick in his mouth. "I don't hear you talkin' that G-shit no more, pussy," I said, then turned toward Falon. "Bitch, you knew from the jump. You were in on it 'cause Boobie ain't wanna wife yo' slut-ass," I spat at her.

"Marshawn, no! I swear on my life, I didn't!" she jumped off the couch, pleading.

"Bitch, you have no life," I sentenced her to death.

Her eyez got wide as realization set in.

Kaboom!

Her body flew back on the couch, then slid halfway down to the floor. Her eyez went blank. She was dead.

Gotti walked over and hit her once more. *Kaboom!* Then he hit Joe in the stomach, too. *Kaboom!* The house went silent as their souls transported to the afterlife.

I noticed the gauge shot forced Joe's dick to fall out of his mouth. I picked it back up and stuffed it back in. I felt no remorse and showed no mercy.

I looked up at the ceiling. "Rest in peace, my nigga. It's over now. We got 'em," I called out to Boobie.

I looked at the mess we made one more time, then got the hell up outta there. I felt the weight leave my shoulders as we walked into the night air.

When I made it home, I went straight to the bathroom so I could shower and wash off that traitor's blood. *Bitch-ass muthafucka.* I wanted to drive back over there and stab his ass again. *Gon' tell me to suck his dick,* I fumed as I stared at myself in the mirror. I couldn't help but notice I looked like some type of demon. My eyez were pitch black with specks of blood on my face. My hoodie and pants had blood all over them. I looked like a survivor in a horror movie.

Olay walked in and caught me staring at myself like a maniac. "Mar-Mar won't go to sleep until you kiss him goodnight," she said.

"After I shower," I replied dryly.

"Ew, you're soaked in blood. What the hell did you just do, Marshawn?" she squealed.

I stripped down and jumped in the shower without responding or lookin' at her. I wasn't ready to look her in the eyez yet. I knew what was to come.

My phone getting blown up back-to-back is what woke me up early the next morning. I seen Burnside's name on the screen and knew what time it was. My heart skipped a beat as I answered.

"What's Mobbin'?" I answered.

"They killed Joe and Falon! The cops got everything

blocked off!'" he yelled in my ear.

"Say what?" I played dumb.

"Get over here to Falon house! They both dead! They killed my nigga!" I could hear the tears in his voice.

"I'm on the way." I hung up.

I rolled out the bed feelin' like a piece of shit and a snake. I didn't know how Joe did it so long, 'cause it didn't feel right. *I ain't no real snake like him.*

"What's wrong, daddy?" Olay sat up, lookin' worried.

"I'll tell you later. Just stay home," I said, then left.

I pulled up at the crime scene, and it looked like the whole block was outside tryna see what happened. It was hella police cars and an ambulance parked in the front. I bounced out and made my way over to my niggaz, who were grouped up right behind the yellow tape. They all looked sick, but none worse than Burnside.

"What's the verdict?" I asked while I gave him a G-hug.

"They both in there dead, Blood. Those bitch-ass house niggaz talkin' 'bout somebody cut Joe dick off and stuffed it in his mouth. They actually enjoyed telling us the details! I'm telling you, O, I'ma end up murdering one of those pussies," he spat. I could see the pain in his eyez.

I made eye contact with Gotti, Bleed, and Twin. I could tell we were all thinking the same thing. We weren't prepared for this part. Beast and Premo looked like they were ready to kill everybody out there.

The house niggaz came back outside and walked right up on us. "Y'all wanna tell us who did this so we can do our jobs, or do y'all wanna finish with your 100 day and night bullshit? 'Cause from the looks of things in there, y'all might wanna call a truce," Detective Rogers said with a smirk.

"Wanna be funny?" Burnside stepped up into their faces, ready to take it there.

"Y'all still wanna shoot at cops?" he shot back, still sore about the situation at Irvington Park.

"Actually, yeah, but this time we won't miss," Burnside said, stepping even closer in their faces.

"Is that a threat, punk?" Rogers gritted his teeth.

Beast and Premo stepped closer, ready for whatever. A few cops peeped the situation and started walking up, also. I knew it could pop off at any moment, given the extra stress and emotions runnin' high like they were. I grabbed Burnside by the arm and whispered in his ear.

"Not right now. We can't win this one. Stop acting off emotions and act like the street general that you are."

He nodded at me, then let me pull him toward my car. All eyez were on us as we walked to the car. I could hear people whispering our names as we walked by. They acted like they didn't have nothin' better to do. *Vultures.*

"You 'bout to have us shootin' it out with the SWAT team over yo' ego. Is you good, my nigga?" I asked as soon as we got in the car.

"Hell naw, I ain't coo', nigga! That's my muthafuckin' favorite relative dead up in there. Bitch-ass pigs tryna play me for a sucka. I'm ready to die about it! I'm telling you, O, I'm 'bout to get on some real murder shit, my nigga. Anybody that's ever disrespected us or owes us money or fuckz with them niggaz is dead! You hear me, O? They're fuckin' dead. I'm killin' dawgs and children about this one, and that's on my mother's grave, O. Ain't no calming me down, so don't even try that shit, either," he said, full of pain. The tears were runnin' down his face now.

"We're going to get the niggaz that did this. You already know that. But you can't be out here movin' off of emotions and have the whole team sitting in prison. We gotta use our heads, brody," I tried to reason with him.

He sat there wiping his face and tryna gain his composure. His body was shaking with anger. I could feel the hate radiating from his pores.

"I'ma kill these niggaz," he promised with a vengeance.

His words gave me the chillz. It was at that moment I knew we made the right decision not telling him about Joe. There was no way he was going to just let us kill his family. The love was too strong, too real. As much as it pained me, I knew it was the right move. Joe had left us no alternative. *Bosses make the hardest choices,* I told myself.

Right when I was getting ready to respond, I saw Olay's Range Rover drive past us. *What the fuck!*

"C'mon, there go Olay," I said, then hopped out. I got to the car just as she was getting out. I looked through the window and saw my son watching his tablet. I wrapped Olay up in a bear hug. "I told you to stay home, baby," I told her.

"Is she really dead, Marshawn?" She broke down cryin' in my arms.

A loud commotion caused me to turn my head toward the front of the house. *Aw, shit,* I thought as I watched the paramedics bring the bodies out on stretchers.

Olay broke free from me and ran toward the crowd. I didn't even try to stop her. I just let her go. By the time I made it over, they had managed to pull the zippers down on the black bags. Everybody screwed their faces up in disgust. Olay let out a cry that sounded like it came from her soul, then she fell to the ground and balled up, cryin' her eyez out.

Hearing her wail like that really fucked with my heart. That was the first time in a long time I regretted somethin' I did. *I should've let her live,* I told myself as I scooped Olay up and carried her to the car.

I knew darker days for my family were in the near future. I knew Olay was going to be heartbroken for years behind her sister. I knew it was going to be damn near impossible to stop Burnside from going on a warpath. Between him and his two cousins from New Jersey, I knew a whole lot of blood was about to be spilled.

My only concern was making sure the truth never got out. I wasn't too worried about it, though, 'cause the niggaz I went in that house with would never tell a soul. The plan was to take that secret to the grave with us.

Jersey Joe had played a dangerous game and lost. *Fuck that nigga.*

Marcellus Allen

Chapter 16

A Few Days Later

I listened to the preacher talk about Falon's life like he knew her, which he didn't. Then he moved on to Joe, which he really didn't know. I had to block the bullshit out 'cause it was starting to become too much. Since Joe didn't have much family in Portland, his body was being shipped back to Jersey so his family could do the funeral there.

It was already a few more funerals scheduled for next week thanks to Burnside and his cousins. I don't think they even got a few hours of sleep since Joe died. Those niggaz were crushin' everything moving! They had the city walkin' on eggshells. They took 100 days, 100 nights to another level. I jumped out there a few times myself, but was more concerned with stackin' my money back up.

After this pretty, light-skinned chick got through singing, it was time to view the body. I had no plans on going up there, but Olay was cryin' and begging me to walk with her. "A'ight, come on." I gave up and walked with her hand-in-hand.

Falon looked at peace in the coffin, like she was just sleeping. The gauge didn't hit her face, so she really didn't look bad. That was the least we could do, give her family an open casket.

Olay broke down cryin' again and hid her face in my chest. I just stared at her and felt some regret shoot through my body. *Damn, girl, you weren't supposed to snake us like that,* I thought.

I walked Olay back to her seat, feeling like a snake my damn self. I was getting way too hot in my suit. I told Olay I had to get some fresh air.

When I stepped outside, the whole crew was out there, posted up just in case the enemies tried to slide by. They had all paid their respects, then got up outta there. Burnside looked like he was hoping somebody had the heart to come through.

"Phatz, rock with me really quick," I told him.

"Where you 'bout to go?" Gotti asked.

"Take a quick drive, get some fresh air. Y'all hold it down. I'll be right back." I dapped everybody up before peeling off.

I put on that *Miss My Dawg* by Lil Wayne and just rode out. I was sick my nigga was dead, but I was glad we got the sucka that did it. *Life is crazy,* I thought while shaking my head. I looked over at Phatz and smiled to myself. He was wearing a shit bag and was still out in the mix. He had really made me respect his gangsta the last few months.

I parked inside the cemetery and killed the engine. "I'll be right back. I got a promise I gotta keep," I told Phatz.

"Tell the homie I'm out here ridin' hard for 'im. Tell 'im I said I'll never let him down, ever." He said it like he meant it.

"I gotchu." Then I made that slow walk to my nigga's grave.

"I'm back, my nigga, just like I said I would. We torched that pussy Joe for what he did to you. We did him real greezy, too. Cut his dick off and everything. That bitch Falon was the main reason why he did what he did. We crushed her raspy-ass, too, on me. Man, shit ain't the same since you been gone, brody." It started raining real hard outta nowhere. I crouched down so I felt closer to my nigga. "I'ma hold you down forever, my nigga. Keep a room ready for me, 'cause this Earth shit ain't all what it's cracked up to be. I'll tap back in later. Gone!" I kissed his headstone and jogged back to the car.

I drove back to the funeral with a heavy heart. The game was really starting to wear my soul down.

"I wish I coulda' been there to pop Joe's bitch-ass. Ol' traitor-ass punk. Over some pussy!" Phatz said as we were pulling back up.

I know he wanted me to reply, but I couldn't. I was too emotionally drained. Plus, outside of what he did to Boobie, Joe was my nigga. It hurt me to have to crush him like that, but it was always the ones closest to you that hurt you the most.

"Go get my wife for me, brody. I can't go back in there. That woman was like a li'l sister to me," I said instead.

"A'ight, I got you," he said, then opened the door, but turned around to me when he got one foot out. "You did the right thing, bro," he finished, then went into the church.

***

It was that time. The time we had all been waiting for. We had Butta dead to rights, and we came to eat. We were hungry.

I sat in the back seat, loading up the Draco with my baseball gloves on. *I'ma torch this nigga,* I promised myself as I loaded the last three bullets in the thirty-round clip.

Click! Click!

I was ready to purge the Earth of the fat nigga. It was a long time coming. His bitch-ass had the heart to go on a double-date to the movie theater across the street from the Lloyd Center Mall. I don't know what movie they went to see, but it was gon' cost him his life. We were four-deep in a blacked-out Impala parked a few spots down from his blue Benz. The same one he was driving when they shot me and grazed my bitch in the head. I felt my blood boil.

"I can't believe yo' li'l bitch just happened to spot this ho-nigga," I said to Beast, who was sitting next to me in the back seat.

"Yeah, son. The Devil says it's time to bring him home," Beast replied. The anger was apparent in his voice.

"He need to hurry up so I can kill his bitch-ass for what he did to Joe, word is bond," Premo added from the passenger seat.

My heart skipped a beat at the mention of Joe's name, like it always did. For some reason I always felt like it was coming back to haunt me. There had been a lot of speculation and rumors around his death. We even heard about a few people taking credit for it that made no sense at all, but what didn't happen was the Gutta Squad taking credit for it like they usually did. They shot some subliminal about it, but didn't actually take the credit. Maybe 'cause their main internet thug, Pull Out, was dead. Either way, Butta and Pressha were going to be my scapegoats.

"Here come a bunch of people. The movies must be over," Burnside said, turning down Li'l Boosie's BooPac album.

I sat up, fully alert, and started watching everybody, scanning the crowd. It took a few minutes, then we finally saw those two pussies walking toward us with their bitches. I didn't know the one with Pressha, but recognized the other as Butta's baby mama.

"That's Butta baby mama that's walkin' with him," I told the group.

"Good, 'cause we killin' that ho, too! We crushin' all of them for Joe," Burnside spat.

Take a deep breath. I know what I'm doing.

We all bounced out at the same time, guns drawn. I didn't

wear no mask. I wanted them niggas to look at me before they left the Earth.

I saw Pressha's eyez get wide as he froze for a split second.

"What's up now, niggaz?" I yelled out, then got to bustin'.

Doom! Doom! Doom! Doom!

Boom! Boom!

Boc! Boc! Boc!

Boom! Boom!

Pressha pushed his chick in front of him to take his bullets for him, and take them she did. She looked like she was break dancin' before finally hitting the ground. That gave Pressha enough time to pull his Tech and get to bustin'.

Taat! Taat! Taat!

Boom! Boom! Boom! Boom!

Doom! Doom!

Boc! Boc!

Butta pulled out some li'l-ass handgun that was only gon' get 'im killed. He was determined to go out with a bang, though.

Pressha ran behind a car for cover and kept waving that Tech at us. We spread out to dodge the hot shit he was sending our way, then lit that car up. *Yeah, nigga, don't hide.*

I saw Butta's baby mama making a run for it, then she got dropped like she took a couple to the legs. Butta wanted to be Captain Save-A-Ho and tried to help her up while still serving us. We torched his ass, and I know one of my .223 bullets had to be the one that dropped him. He fell on his side, hittin' the pavement hard. *Man down!* I watched his gun fly, then hit the ground, sliding out of his reach.

Boom! Boom! Boom!

Boc! Boc!

Doom! Doom! Doom!

We got to eatin' Pressha's ass up behind that car. We spread out, then circled the car like we were a part of the Marines or somethin'. Pressha was laid out on the ground with blood oozing from his stomach and mouth. His gun was still in his hand, but he was having too much trouble breathing to do anything with it.

"Breathe, dawg. You gotta breathe," I taunted him. I'd been waiting far too long for this kill not to savor it. I smiled down at him.

"This for Joe, bitch!" Burnside yelled.

"I wish we woulda killed his bitch-ass. Fuck Joe, and fuck slobs." He spat out blood, then tried to lift his gun.

Doom! Doom!

Boom!

Boc! Boc!

Boom! Boom!

We filled him up with lead and had his head bouncing like a basketball. He was no longer.

"Help!" we heard a female scream out. It was Butta's baby mama crawling and looking for help.

Beast went and kicked her in the stomach, making her flip on her back.

"Please! I've got kids!" she pleaded.

"They'll miss you," he stated, real calm-like.

Boom! Boom! Boom! Boom! Boom!

Click!

He emptied his clip, then she departed from this earth.

We ran over to Butta, who was barely alive. He was moaning like a sucka.

"I know you ain't tryna play possum," Burnside taunted.

"Fuck you, nigga. You better kill me," he whispered. Like we wasn't. Like that wasn't why we had come in the first place.

Burnside crouched down and stuck his gun in his mouth. He stared right in his eyez like the killer he was.

Boom!

He blew the inside of his mouth and his brains out, never breaking eye contact. He slowly stood, then looked at me with those devil eyez. "He said he was the king of Portland," he reminded me, then we was outta there.

Real Shooters by Li'l Boosie was playing when we hopped in.

***

One Month Later

I was driving Tamia to her doctor's appointment, so we could have the baby checked up on. I had to take her crazy-ass once a month. She was eight months pregnant and more than ready to drop the load. I couldn't wait, either. I was dyin' to meet my li'l princess.

It definitely started off as a good day. The weather was nice, and the last couple of days had been drama-free. 100 days, 100 nights was still in effect, but was dyin' down. I was falling back and tryna build my empire up. The only niggaz that were tryna take it there with us were the Sixties, and I planned on crushin' them as soon as the heat died down. It was undisputed who the king of Portland was and what crew was in charge.

"What's Mobbin'? I answered my phone.

"Yo', the nigga Burnside said it's an emergency that you get over here to the studio," Bleed said.

"Man, I'm on the way to the doctor's appointment with Tamia right now. Whatever it is, just have Gotti handle it," I replied, getting irritated.

"Gotti ain't been answering all day, brody," Burnside said. "It's a level five emergency."

Aw, shit! "A'ight, I'm on the way, Blood. And where the fuck is Burnside at?"

"He said he on the way right now."

"I'll be there in, like, ten minutes." I hung up on him. Somethin' in my gut was tryna tell me it was all bad. *What the fuck is going on?* I called Burnside to get some answers.

"What's Mobbin'?" he answered.

"What's the triv? Let me know right now. You know I hate feeling blindsided and shit," I told him.

"I can't say it over the phone, bro. It's way too hot. I'm on my way there now, too. But if you get there before me, it's a Toyota Camry parked in the lot. The emergency is in the trunk," he said.

"A'ight, I'm on it." I hung up feeling more confused than I originally was. "Baby, I'ma have to drop you off at the doctor's by yourself, but I promise I'll make it back." I looked over at Tamia.

She looked at me like I was delusional. "No, the hell you ain't 'bout to drop me off! I'm going with you, then we'll go to the doctor's together. Uh-uh, I ain't going for that shit," she shot me down.

I didn't feel like arguing with no pregnant bitch, so I busted a U-turn and headed to the spot. The whole way there I knew something was wrong. I could feel it. *Burnside done got us into some shit,* I thought.

When I finally pulled up, everybody was waiting outside. Bleed, Phatz, Twin, and even Rugar. Even he was on high alert. I jumped out with my hands in the air, showing my frustration. "Where the hell Burnside at?" I asked the group

"Not here yet," Bleed answered.

"Fuck it. Let's go open this trunk and see what the fuck he done got us into now," I replied. I could smell the scent of a dead body coming from the trunk within ten feet of the car. That's when I knew it was bad.

"What the fuck is that smell?" Bleed asked the obvious.

"Pop the trunk so we can see what his nigga done got us into," I told him.

He opened the trunk real slow, like he was scared or somethin'. I got more anxious every second, and then my life changed.

"What the fuck!" Bleed yelled, then jumped back lookin' like he'd seen a ghost.

The rest of us came forward to see what had him so shook up. What I seen made me wanna throw up. Gotti was staring up at us with half of his face blown off. My nigga was dead to this world. The nigga who was like a big brother to me was staring at me with lifeless eyez.

I grabbed the paper that was sticking outta his mouth and read it out loud. "You took my favorite relative from me, now I took yours. So, obviously, ain't nothin' to talk about. We're at war now! 'Lord, protect me from my friends. I can take care of my enemies.' P.S. One life, one love, so there can only be one king," I read the venom.

"It's wartime, dawg," Twin said. He looked ready, like he had been expecting this.

"How he find out?" Bleed wondered out loud what I was thinking.

I shook my head while evils spread throughout my veins. I was going to war with the most dangerous nigga I knew. 'Lord, protect me from my friends.'

I'ma need it, I thought.

To Be Continued...
Steady Mobbin' 3
Coming Soon

Submission Guideline

Submit the first three chapters of your completed manuscript to ldpsubmissions@gmail.com, subject line: Your book's title. The manuscript must be in a .doc file and sent as an attachment. Document should be in Times New Roman, double spaced and in size 12 font. Also, provide your synopsis and full contact information. If sending multiple submissions, they must each be in a separate email.

Have a story but no way to send it electronically? You can still submit to LDP/Ca$h Presents. Send in the first three chapters, written or typed, of your completed manuscript to:

LDP: Submissions Dept
Po Box 870494
Mesquite, Tx 75187

DO NOT send original manuscript. Must be a duplicate.

Provide your synopsis and a cover letter containing your full contact information.

Thanks for considering LDP and Ca$h Presents.

Coming Soon from Lock Down Publications/Ca$h Presents

BOW DOWN TO MY GANGSTA

By **Ca$h**

TORN BETWEEN TWO

By **Coffee**

BLOOD STAINS OF A SHOTTA **III**

By **Jamaica**

STEADY MOBBIN II

By **Marcellus Allen**

BLOOD OF A BOSS **V**

By **Askari**

LOYAL TO THE GAME **IV**

By **T.J. & Jelissa**

A DOPEBOY'S PRAYER **II**

By **Eddie "Wolf" Lee**

IF LOVING YOU IS WRONG... **III**

LOVE ME EVEN WHEN IT HURTS

By **Jelissa**

TRUE SAVAGE **V**

By **Chris Green**

BLAST FOR ME **III**

By **Ghost**

ADDICTIED TO THE DRAMA **III**

By **Jamila Mathis**

LIPSTICK KILLAH **III**

CRIME OF PASSION **II**

By **Mimi**

WHAT BAD BITCHES DO **III**

KILL ZONE

By **Aryanna**

THE COST OF LOYALTY **II**

By **Kweli**

SHE FELL IN LOVE WITH A REAL ONE **II**

By **Tamara Butler**

LOVE SHOULDN'T HURT **III**

RENEGADE BOYS **II**

By **Meesha**

CORRUPTED BY A GANGSTA **III**

By **Destiny Skai**

A GANGSTER'S CODE III

By **J-Blunt**

KING OF NEW YORK III

By **T.J. Edwards**

CUM FOR ME **IV**

By **Ca$h & Company**

GORILLAS IN THE BAY

De'Kari

THE STREETS ARE CALLING

Duquie Wilson

KINGPIN KILLAZ II

Hood Rich

STEADY MOBBIN' 3

Marcellus Allen

Available Now

RESTRAINING ORDER **I & II**

By **CA$H & Coffee**

LOVE KNOWS NO BOUNDARIES **I II & III**

By **Coffee**

RAISED AS A GOON I, II, III & IV

BRED BY THE SLUMS I, II, III

BLAST FOR ME I & II

ROTTEN TO THE CORE I III

By **Ghost**

LAY IT DOWN **I & II**

LAST OF A DYING BREED

BLOOD STAINS OF A SHOTTA I & II

By **Jamaica**

LOYAL TO THE GAME

LOYAL TO THE GAME II

LOYAL TO THE GAME III

By **TJ & Jelissa**

BLOODY COMMAS I & II

SKI MASK CARTEL I II & III

KING OF NEW YORK I II

By **T.J. Edwards**

IF LOVING HIM IS WRONG…I & II

By **Jelissa**

WHEN THE STREETS CLAP BACK I & II III

By **Jibril Williams**

A DISTINGUISHED THUG STOLE MY HEART I II & III

LOVE SHOULDN'T HURT I II

RENEGADE BOYS

By **Meesha**

A GANGSTER'S CODE I & II

By J-Blunt

PUSH IT TO THE LIMIT

By **Bre' Hayes**

BLOOD OF A BOSS **I, II, III & IV**

By **Askari**

THE STREETS BLEED MURDER **I, II & III**

THE HEART OF A GANGSTA I II& III

By **Jerry Jackson**

CUM FOR ME

CUM FOR ME 2

CUM FOR ME 3

An **LDP Erotica Collaboration**

BRIDE OF A HUSTLA **I II & II**

THE FETTI GIRLS **I, II& III**

CORRUPTED BY A GANGSTA I & II

By **Destiny Skai**

WHEN A GOOD GIRL GOES BAD

By **Adrienne**

A GANGSTER'S REVENGE **I II III & IV**

THE BOSS MAN'S DAUGHTERS

THE BOSS MAN'S DAUGHTERS II

Marcellus Allen

THE BOSSMAN'S DAUGHTERS III
THE BOSSMAN'S DAUGHTERS IV
THE BOSS MAN'S DAUGHTERS **V**
A SAVAGE LOVE **I & II**
BAE BELONGS TO ME
A HUSTLER'S DECEIT I, II
WHAT BAD BITCHES DO I, II
By **Aryanna**
A KINGPIN'S AMBITON
A KINGPIN'S AMBITION **II**
I MURDER FOR THE DOUGH
By **Ambitious**
TRUE SAVAGE
TRUE SAVAGE II
TRUE SAVAGE **III**
TRUE SAVAGE **IV**
By **Chris Green**
A DOPEBOY'S PRAYER
By **Eddie "Wolf" Lee**
THE KING CARTEL **I, II & III**
By **Frank Gresham**
THESE NIGGAS AIN'T LOYAL **I, II & III**
By **Nikki Tee**
GANGSTA SHYT **I II &III**
By **CATO**
THE ULTIMATE BETRAYAL
By **Phoenix**

204

BOSS'N UP **I , II & III**
By **Royal Nicole**
I LOVE YOU TO DEATH
By Destiny J
I RIDE FOR MY HITTA
I STILL RIDE FOR MY HITTA
By **Misty Holt**
LOVE & CHASIN' PAPER
By **Qay Crockett**
TO DIE IN VAIN
By **ASAD**
BROOKLYN HUSTLAZ
By **Boogsy Morina**
BROOKLYN ON LOCK I & II
By **Sonovia**
GANGSTA CITY
By **Teddy Duke**
A DRUG KING AND HIS DIAMOND I & II III
A DOPEMAN'S RICHES
By Nicole Goosby
TRAPHOUSE KING **I II & III**
KINGPIN KILLAZ
By **Hood Rich**
LIPSTICK KILLAH **I, II**
CRIME OF PASSION
By **Mimi**
STEADY MOBBN' I, II

By **Marcellus Allen**

<u>WHO SHOT YA **I, II**</u>

Renta

BOOKS BY LDP'S CEO, CA$H

TRUST IN NO MAN

TRUST IN NO MAN 2

TRUST IN NO MAN 3

BONDED BY BLOOD

SHORTY GOT A THUG

THUGS CRY

THUGS CRY 2

THUGS CRY 3

TRUST NO BITCH

TRUST NO BITCH 2

TRUST NO BITCH 3

TIL MY CASKET DROPS

RESTRAINING ORDER

RESTRAINING ORDER 2

IN LOVE WITH A CONVICT

Coming Soon

BONDED BY BLOOD 2

BOW DOWN TO MY GANGSTA

Marcellus Allen